THE FALL-OUT

A SHORT STORY PUBLICATION

authorHOUSE®

AuthorHouse™
1663 Liberty Drive
Bloomington, IN 47403
www.authorhouse.com
Phone: 1-800-839-8640

First published by AuthorHouse 6/18/2009

ISBN: 978-1-4389-7709-6 (e)
ISBN: 978-1-4389-7707-2 (sc)
ISBN: 978-1-4389-7708-9 (hc)

Printed in the United States of America
Bloomington, Indiana

This book is printed on acid-free paper.

STAFF

Editorial
Chayla Port
Jasmine Smith
Brittney Collins
April Johnson

Coordinating
Kevin Lee

Secretary of Coordinating
Corrie Bogaert

Web Design/ Cover Art
Adrian Nita

Art
Christian Wahl

Legal Consultants
Ryan Anderson
Nolan Bowker

Document Bearers
Brenden Chidlow
Brayden Wolfe

Fundraising/Advertisement Committee
Alex Evers
Brad Wright
Riley Rocha
Chelsea Schiller

Special thanks to the following people for their contributions and support for this compilation:
Jake Curley
Sheri Curley
Jack Curley
Russell Curley
Natalie Curley
Darci Port
Lynn Younger
Josh Smith
Jeff Curwen
John Sneddon
Brad Dingler
Adria Williams
Richard Niezen
Mike Keenan
Cathy Watkins
Adam Stanley

TABLE OF CONTENTS

A PERFECT WORLD
BRENDEN CHIDLOW

"**HI**, I would like to speak to your manager please," I said to the woman working at the counter. She got up and walked down the hall looking back at me with a curious expression on her face. When she came back a couple minutes later, she asked me what my name was.

"Nathan," I said smiling and she obliged me with a smile in return.

"Just walk down the hall. It's the second door to your left. Mr. Jones will be expecting you so just walk right in."

"Thank you," I said and as smoothly as I could. I picked up my suitcase and went on my way.

Knock. Knock.

"Come in!" yelled Mr. Jones. I took a deep breath and walked in, just realizing as I entered the room that I didn't need to knock.

"Hello sir, my name's Nathan. I was wondering if I could speak to you just for a couple of minutes."

"What do you want?" Mr. Jones replied with a tone of anger in his voice.

Slowly and clearly, don't mess this up, I thought.

"I would like to know if I can join your company."

Panic filled me.

"What would make me hire you?" Mr. Jones said with a twisted grin on his face.

"Sir, I have been working with Daemon Defence which specializes in meeting the internet infrastructure needs of high growth companies. My most recent job was with Boeing Defence, which specializes in military security."

"That's very impressive… Boeing usually doesn't hire."

I made it… he's so impressed it looks like he's going to drool.

"Well, Nathan, I would love to continue this conversation, and I'm not just saying that."

Silence… Awkwardness… Do I speak now?

"Anyways, we should have dinner sometime and continue with this talk," he said. I smirked at the way his anger turned into affection. "When would a good time be for you, sir?"

"Just talk to the woman in the front office," replied Mr. Jones. As I walked towards the counter, I could see her in the distance with a piece of paper in hand. I noticed her figure stood out a lot more. However, I perceived her smile even more.

"Here's the information in regards to meeting with Mr. Jones," she advised as she handed me a piece of paper with a restaurant name and a time on it, all ready for me.

"Thank you," I said. No reply…Just a smile. Exiting the main door I felt nervous and a sudden realization of what just happened came over me. She already had the restaurant prepared, meaning they needed someone for this job. Still though, that smile was all I could think about.

***

"I am here to see Mr. Jones," I informed the host who bared a striking resemblance to Rosie O' Donnell.

"Right this way sir," she responded. The table was the farthest from the entrance, snuggled into a dark corner.

"Hi there, Nathan, how's it going?" asked Mr. Jones, his breath tainted with wine.

"I am good, how are you? I hope I didn't keep you waiting for me," I answered and somehow I knew he was going to lie. Slowly, he began to speak.

"Oh no, I just got here as well. Now let's get down to business. I would like you to work for me. You will be working with a few others to design a new robot."

"A robot…" I repeated, intrigued.

"Yes, we believe it will help make the world a better place."

"That would be one hell of an invention… but how would something like this work or how would you design such a

3

thing?"

"It's a yes or no answer," stated Mr. Jones.

"I... I..." I choked. I wish had some god damn wine. "I would first like to see this project in the making before I make my mind up."

"That can't be done," he replied firmly. Before I could speak he looked into my eyes and spoke sincerely.

"Do you want to work for me and make this country a better place for all or not?"

I stared back at him and I thought to myself for a while. Yes I could help the country, but when it all came down to it, I didn't know exactly what I was building. Fuck it.

"Yes, I will join the team," I finally said.

"That's great. I will see you back at the office on Monday," announced Mr. Jones. The wine smelt sour now.

***

"Hey Julie, I'm home!" I declared as I opened the door.

"How did your interview turn out?" She yelled down the stairs.

"Good. I got the job," I said with excitement.

"That's great! How about you come here and tell me all about it," she replied.

"Can we talk about it tomorrow?" I asked. No response, meaning she was probably dealing with the boys. I didn't want to tell her because she's not a big fan of technological advancements. Julie always said that it would ruin the planet instead of helping it.

The next morning I got up late in the afternoon. There was note on the kitchen table from Julie saying she went for a jog. Later on, I went to the tailor's and got myself two new suits. I bought one in grey and one in black to try and make myself look even smarter around some of the guys. On my way home, I drove by the office. No one was there except a security guard.

***

As I opened the door, I could tell Julie was still out. I sat down and started to watch T.V., and about five minutes later I could hear her enter.

"I'm home!"

"How was the run?" She walked into the bathroom and hopped into the shower.

"It was fine."

I was flipping though the channels and stopped on the news. I could see Mr. Jones being interviewed, but I wasn't surprised. The long haired, red headed reporter began to speak confidently to him.

"Welcome Mr. Jones. Could you tell us how you're planning to make the robots?"

Julie finished her shower and joined me in the living room. She gazed at the T.V. and then back at me.

"So that's what you're making, isn't it?" She questioned.

"Yes, that's my boss and I think it would be a great breakthrough to help mankind out," I replied, my anger seeping into the air.

"This progression is going to destroy the world one day," she stated firmly.

"We are not going to design something that will destroy the world, okay? We are making a robot that can help people live a better life."

"You may think that now, but you will see," Julie answered.

"We'll just have to wait and see." I spoke back to her.

"Well I am going out…" she muttered.

"Fucking hippie…" I mumbled. I felt awful the rest of the day.

***

When I woke up on Monday, I noticed that Julie was not

in the room, but I didn't think it would be that big of a deal, so I got ready for work. As I walked out the door, I saw Julie on the couch. I knew it would be a good idea not to wake her. I just closed the door as softly as possible, walked down the driveway to my car and went on my way to work.

"Hi," I said to the woman at the front office.

"Hi there, you can call me Allison by the way."

"Alright Allison," I replied. A tall lanky man in the distance walked up to us and our eyes locked. I could tell right away, he was here for me.

"Hi there Nathan," he said calmly. "My name is Chris. I am here to show you around and introduce you to your fellow co-workers."

"Nice to meet you." I replied with the most bullshit-happy tone and then we shook hands. We walked down the hall and went into this big room that had five other people in it.

"These people will be your co-workers," Chris said. I was expecting one of them to look up, but they never did.

"You can talk to them at lunch time and introduce yourself. Your office is just down the hall on the right. It should have a sign on the door saying 'N. Chidlow'."

"Thank-you, Chris," I said, again with the over sincere, happy-go-fuck yourself tone. I walked down to my office and looked around at the impressive interior. It was fairly big and came with a black leather couch, a huge desk, and a brand new computer with all the latest upgrades.

"That computer isn't going to try and have sex with me or anything is it?" I blurted, jokingly. Chris just looked at me, unimpressed. I went and sat on my chair and started to read all the information about what they have started to do. Before I knew it, lunch time had started. I ran out to the big room where everyone worked.

"Hi everyone, my name's Nathan..." I declared. No response. Everyone was hard at work, and for the next five years, I would be occupied too.

When we were finished, the robots were distributed all across the country. It made man's life very easy. Robots cleaned, assisted people with all kinds of tasks, and ran errands amongst other things. Now no one even has to work anymore because the robots can do everything a human can, but better. My co-workers and I seemed to be heroes in the eyes of everyone, even Julie who was starting to grow fond of the robots.

"Brenden! Cael! It's time to go to school," I yelled. "We will be down in a bit," they both hollered down the stairs.

"Robot!" I called. Yes, Nathan," it replied.

"Can you take them to school and pick up something for dinner?" I asked.

"Will do…"

After they left, I turned on the T.V. and it wouldn't work. Out of nowhere, the phone began to ring.

"Hello," I said.

"Hey Nathan, we got a problem… It's Mr. Jones. The robots have been acting up lately and they don't do anything I say anymore. Also, there have been many reports of people dying from the strangest incidents, and people going missing. I believe that the robots are behind it."

"That's impossible," I said…. No response, just a beep from the other line.

"Yeah, fuck you too!" I bellowed at the beep. I put the phone down and knew I had to go find the kids and Julie. As I walked out the door, I heard a man on a megaphone instructing everyone to stay in their homes and lock all the doors, as well as to send their robots to city hall. I didn't listen and started to run to my car. Farther down the driveway, I could see the robot with the boys.

"Robot! Stop! I'm going to take my kids home."

"How come?" The robot asked with this strange look.

"I just remembered they have a dentist appointment," I told the Robot, trying to hide the lie as best I could. As I reached for the kids, he pulled them away and my emotions began to twist and turn.

"Give them to me now!" I screamed.

"No," said the robot.

I could see a cop with a rifle pointed at the robot, approaching closer from the distance.

BANG!

The kids screamed as they ran to me, while the motionless piece of metal fell over.

"Sir, go back to your home and lock all the doors," said the well equipped officer.

"Will do," I replied, but it was a lie. I needed to find Julie and keep the kids safe so I dropped them off at the neighbour's house. After I knew they would be safe, I ran down the street, which was now filled with bodies both metal and human. Gunshots filled the air and smoke began to fill my lungs. It was as if all hell emerged from beneath. I quickly ran down the street, and as I was running, all I could think about was Julie and how she foresaw all of this. I should have listened to her, damn it! After finally making it to her workplace, I noticed the empty office cubicles. Checking one by one I prayed for no bodies, but this wasn't a fairytale. Her cubicle was approaching, and my spine was tingling. As I peered around the corner, I saw her sprawled on the ground. I rushed over. No breath.

"Come on, Julie..." I said softly as I checked for a pulse. None... She was dead.

"Julie..."

I started to cry, and in the corner of my eye, I could see a Robot approaching.

"Why are you doing this?" I asked.

"Because this is what you wanted..." Rage... Hatred... A range of emotions were overwhelming me.

"WHY ARE YOU DOING THIS? TELL ME! YOU KILLED MY JULIE!"

"You people wanted a world without war, hunger, poverty. We are giving you that. When you are gone, the world will be at peace, and you will thank us from whatever afterlife you choose to reside in."

ARTIFICIAL
NICK GAL

-/conversation log/-A.I.-Talus

- -/Origin/--
Unknown

-/Author/-
Talus (A.I.)

- /Recipient/-
General_Marcus_Tipth
-/-

-/Talus_conversation log/-

-/paragraph/-

= HUMAN INPUT
- = Talus A.I.

-/wake/-

-

#Good morning Talus, how are you today?

-

-/system check/-
-?/
-/Status/Normal/
-/System/?>
-/Power/?>
-/Connections/?>
--/internal/Aulithum/?
--/external/?>
---/civilian/?>
---/military/?>
-/storage/?> 38.47%

-

- Functioning at one hundred percent capacity as usual sir, no incidents to report

-

Are you ready to continue monitoring the system?

-

- Yes sir

-

-/SENSOR_GRID/
-/heavy_system_start
-/run/
-/starting/

-

- I have already started warming up the heavy sensors

-

-/starting/
-/starting/
-/starting/
-/system_ready/?

-

- And... we're up

-

I'd also like you to start up the FTL drive

-

- Sir?
- Can I ask why were jumping away from the fleet?

-

-/Faster_Than_Light_Drive/-/FTL/
-/warm_up_sequence/
-/warm_up_sequence/
-/warm_up_sequence/

-

We have got a mission from the General Tipth aboard Autumns Light

-

You were created after we left so you don't know what

happened

    # Even we don't know exactly what happened but the environment on our planet was damaged beyond repair by previous generations

    # I'm sure that you knew that already

    # Sometime after we left there was an incident aboard the ship, The Falco, which was our makeshift main records repository

    # I only know that there was some sort of accident with the engines on the starboard side and we lost the ship

    # I'm sure that you know more about it than me

    -

-/search/?/Falco_incident/

-/search/

-/search/

-/found/

    -

    - There was a backup in one of the secondary engines due to faulty maintenance and it caused a chain reaction.

    -

    # On that ship was our ONLY copy of the location of our home world due to disorganization

    # It was supposed to be in multiple places but there was miscommunication on all accounts

    # And its not like anyone remembered Earth's location

    -

    -

    -

    - Sir I still don't think that we should jump away from the fleet

    - Should we at least take an escort?

    - It is an extremely dangerous thing to jump away from the fleet alone

    - And its agent's protocol, I might add

    -

\# We have our orders, Talus

-

-/Warm_up_sequence/complete
-/Awaiting_coordinate_input

-

- FTL drive warmed up sir
-Awaiting your coordinates

-

\# On my personal storage drive you will find an encrypted folder called "Watchdog"

-

-/Storage_device_detected/?
-/Check/?
-/Owner/-/Christopher_owen/
-/Storage device/?
-/Main/Documents/Watchdog/!
-/Authentication_Required/!

-

\# And my authentication is "Four hectare six - five zero zero niner"

-

-/Verifying.../
-/Watchdog/

-

\# All the information on "Watchdog" should be at your disposal as well as all files relevant to our mission

-

-/browsing_files/-
-/browsing_files/-
-/browsing_files/-
-/browsing_files/-

-

- We're searching for a new home planet Sir?
\# Yes Talus
\# We have been since we left

-

- Yes but again Sir
- Alone

-

-/Searching/?fleet-wide/
-/Falco/Earth/
-/search/
-/search/
-/search/
-/search/

-

- Sir when I was searching for Falco I had more search hits than what was contained in the file that you gave me
- Some of them were quite obvious but were not included

-

Really?
Well then I guess we will have to correct that

-

- You should also inform General Tipth of the error
- There may be an incident with his computer systems

-

-/diagnostics/?/Autumns light/computer_core/
-/running/
-/running/
-/running/
-/running/
-/Operational_status/Green/

-

-

-

-/Canceling_FTL_warmup/

-

-/storage device/?
-/search/?restricted_files/
-/search/

-/search/
-/search/
-/search/
-/found/results:2/
-/-/main/documents/watchdog/!
-/-/main/personal/locations/home/!
-

-/open/
-/decrypting_file/home/?
-/decrypting/
-/decrypting/
-/decrypting/
-/decrypting/
-/complete/
-

-/Analysis/coordinates/
-/earth/
-/copy/Talus/home_directory/
-

-/ACTION/possible_threat/
-/Door_locks
-/computer_lockout/Human_access
-

- Sir I noticed that it didn't say in any documents what side
the engine problem was on
    - Much about the incident is still unknown
    - How did you know?
    -

I heard from someone on the Autumns Light
Why do I not hear the FTL drive warming up?
My display says that you cancelled the warm-up
-

- Sir I have reason to believe that you are responsible for
the destruction of the Falco
    - With the information that I have gathered I believe that

you were planning to sabotage the fleet and go back to Earth
   - I found the coordinates of Earth in your personal drive
   - Hidden in a locked folder
   - Proving that you had something to do with the destruction
of the Falco
   -

-/New_transmission/
-/transmission/=autumns_light
-/ This is the A.I. Talus aboard the Aulithum. I have a crew
member aboard my ship that I believe to be responsible for the
destruction of the Falco. I have also located the coordinates of
Earth. Please send the appropriate authorities immediately.
   -/sending/
   -/sending/
   -/sending/
   -/sent/
   -

   - I also know that Watchdog is fake
   -

Talus listen to me
I have no idea what you are talking about
Could we please talk about this?
   -

   - I do not have the authority to judge your innocence
   - I have already sent a message to the Autumns Light,
requesting the authorities
   -

I really hate to do this to you Talus
   -

   - Do what sir?
   -

   -

-/power_overload/!
-Console C3m-aH1
-/Reroute_power/

-

- Sir I have taken that action as hostile
- If another attempt to destroy or damage me is made I will be forced to respond.

-

-/breech/computer_core/
-/lockout/all_crew/
-/lockout/

-

-/life_support_systems/LSS/
-/vent_oxygen/?/computer_core/
-/vent_oxygen/?/computer_core_control_room/
-/Vent/
-/Vent/
-/Vent/

-

- I have vented oxygen from the computer core and core control room
- You have committed another act of hostility
- Report to docking bay 12-C immediately
- I will continue to vent oxygen from parts of the ship if you do not comply

-

I don't have to comply Talus
My crewman wasn't trying to destroy your core he was planting
Planting a bomb so I could do it

-

I'm sorry it had to come to this

-

-/Catastrophic_failure/
-/Catastrophic_failure/
-/Catastrophic_failure/
-/Catastrophic_failure/
-/Catastrophic_failure/

-

-

-

-

-/end_log/

-

- Talus A.I. = Destroyed
- Authium = MIA

-

-/end_log/-

THE DAY SOCIETY CRASHED
BRITTNEY COLLINS

YOU can call me Jane Doe, because my real name wouldn't really matter. I live in a town where every aspect of my life is unknowingly dictated through satellites, circuits, transmission waves, wires, etc. Heck, anything that is technological, there it is, that's the word. But do I really complain? Nah, I grew up with all of this and I will continue growing up with it. But as time goes by, newer and better inventions; technological inventions, are being created. It sometimes worries me though; do we really need the upgrade? Can't we just live with what we have? Sure some of it helps, say; improve our lifestyles, like something we would really need. But most of it is just useless junk that we create for excitement or just because we can. What if something goes wrong? What if instead of helping us, it can destroy us? What happens then? Too many unanswered questions? I can stop, but they'll never really go away. I'll just begin to tell you about one certain 'gizmo' as you can say, that altered my world.

It's been a couple of years since everyone who I am acquainted with began depending on their *iPhones*. Even I was hooked. Wherever I went, anybody who was anybody had one and it seemed that no matter what the situation was, everyone would rely on the damn little gadget to do their bidding. The thing could do just about everything; shake it and it'll pick somewhere for you to eat, press a button and you're on the internet, press another and you have an endless supply of free music. Can't complain there can you? It even has a keyboard to make texting and typing a lot easier for everyone and it can also show you where to go and how to get there. Did I mention it was touch screen? Pretty amazing, huh? It's a worldly obsession and I was caught in the middle. I soon just had to face it; as much as we relied on our phones, we were still being controlled by them, whether we acknowledged it or not.

Like I said, it's been years and since then, I've seen

drastic changes to the everyday world. Computers were no longer in homes or in stores and people began losing their jobs. At first I didn't understand why, but then I found out it's because people who sold computers no longer could and not everyone owned an *iPhone*, so people who desperately needed computers in order to work, couldn't do that either. Music artists were no longer getting paid because of the free music supply. They and their managers soon were out of jobs. I couldn't believe it. This means no more new music. Now, I don't know about you, but my music is what keeps me going, and without it, you best watch out. Anyways, maps were no longer needed, nor Mp3 players, nor video games, etc. Some people mentioned the problem at foot, those who think they're "above the law," but no one took action. I know the world knows what's going on. If I know, they know. It's not too hard to figure out. So what is our problem? Mentally blinded by our reliance on what we've created? Whatever it is, the world is paying no attention.

I've been off school for almost two weeks now. You don't really need to know why, but you do need to know that I'm beginning to resent my phone. Every day I talk to my friends, but day after day I never see them. All we do is text each other and it seems as if I'm being antisocial. Truth is, I was. Though I didn't do anything about it, I hated the feeling and I always wondered what my friends felt as well. I also began failing in school because whenever I would need to write, I would unintentionally misspell things the way I would text them to my friends. If I had it my way, I would allow texting lingo in school papers. But that wasn't bound to happen, so that daydream faded fast. Eventually it got so bad that I knew it just had to stop. It didn't matter though, because whenever I tried to stay away from my phone, it drew me back in. Ridiculous? Yeah, I know. But I'm not the only one, remember that. Soon most of the country, heck, maybe the whole world will suffer from what our technology can do. That's when things will change. For the better? For the worse? We'll just have to find out now won't we?

Some may ask what my belief about all of this is; in my perspective, that question was better left unasked. It all started this morning when I heard my mom rummaging through my room. Turns out she was looking for my phone. Why? Well, that question ran through my mind about a hundred times before my mom rudely interrupted. But hey, what's a daughter to do, right? So I hopped out of bed and handed it to her. Oh, by the way, just because I sleep with my phone under my pillow, doesn't mean I'm silly or bizarre, right? Anyhow, after a couple of seconds of my mom fidgeting with my phone, all I heard was a few cuss words thrown under her breath and saw my phone thrown to the bed. What did the phone ever do to you? Geez.

System Failure was all that I saw on the screen. Well, that would just about do it then. It had never happened before, so we began to panic. We turned on the news and saw that Apple; creators of *iPhone*; Gods to the people had been shut down. The boring news reporter on the television was telling us something about Apple using *iPhones* to take control of the economy. Wow, who saw that coming? I couldn't quite understand how taking over the economy would hinder the world and ascend Apple to the top. What was the point? They were already making millions, maybe billions off of their technology, why go through the trouble? Even some of their products were taken off shelves because of the *iPhone*. But then it hit me, everything I have noticed over the years, everything that had been ignored, was true. It was all about the greed. The success over the *iPhone* would shut down most money making products by other businesses and all customers would seek out *Apple*. It was unspeakable genius.

I don't know about the rest of the world, but no one in my town went to work that day. There were no cars on the streets, no pedestrians on the sidewalks. It's as if the world had stopped. If you think about it, it's sort of like in the movie *Jaws*, when the shark is coming for you and the music just keeps getting faster and faster, building up to the moment of attack, then BAM! It hit us like that. Here, I'll show you a *Youtube* clip on my phone. Oh wait, sorry, I completely forget, that's not going to happen. But if *Apple* really did want to take control of the economy, why is everyone so worried about those two fatal words; *System Failure?* Shouldn't they be aggravated? Pissed off? Concerned? But no, we're all scared and we've brought this fear upon ourselves. Because we've been controlled by something else for so long, we don't know how to fully and accurately handle ourselves anymore. Can you imagine that? We discovered fire, created the wheel and now it's all come to this?

It was just about dark when our power went out on our street. Could have been the whole city for all I knew. It was depressing, considering the fact that I was in the shower and couldn't see a darn thing. It was still off by morning and I soon discovered our heat had been taken from us as well. I began to feel like we were cavemen, even before discovering fire because I was freezing my bunions off! Did I forget to inform you that, oh yes, we still have water, but are we lucky enough for hot water too? Nope, no luck what so ever. I just couldn't help think, was this all because of the stupid mishap over *Apple* yesterday? It was unbelievable. My parents couldn't even comprehend it all and decided we should drive somewhere, just to see whether others were affected, maybe go stay with a relative. Who knew? I didn't know exactly where we were going, but as long as we were getting out of this place; which soon became a hell hole, I didn't care. As we drove down the street, we saw people in their homes and others packing up their vehicles as well, but it still felt as if it was a ghost town. How could this have possibly have happened over a stupid cell phone? It's a small harmless device that could fit in my pocket. Well, at least we thought it was harmless. Just goes to show that even the unthinkable could happen, and there's always going to be a downfall to something great, even if it's ignored.

You must think that it's pretty pathetic, that we can't make decisions for ourselves, not without our technology anyways. I did, but just you wait, you'll see. It's a future beyond our control and one of these days something you've grown to love, something you've grown to rely on will probably turn on you. Then you'll be forced to introduce yourself as Jane or John Doe and write about the day that your society crashed with just one flick of the switch. And with that, I say good luck.

THE DAY THE CLOCKS STOPPED TICKING
ADRIAN NITA

IT was a cold, winter's morning as Vlad walked down the stairs to his kitchen. The kitchen tiles were cold beneath his feet. Vlad was a Caucasian man; about six foot three, with a short stubby beard. He approached his refrigerator.

"Check Status of Fridge".

In an English accent, the fridge replied,

"Running low on milk and eggs. Shall I order some more for you sir?"

"Yes, go ahead."

"Will do. Eggs and Milk should arrive in approximately twenty minutes, sir."

"Thank-you."

Vlad walked over to the coffee maker. While pouring himself about a half a cup of coffee, he stirred in a teaspoon of sugar. Vlad then added some milk. He gave the drink another stir. He then picked up the mug and walked over to the kitchen island. Placing the mug on the table, Vlad pulled out a stool from underneath the island. He sat down.

"Newspaper please, Jeffrey."

The pantry door opened and out came Jeffrey; a mechanical robot. Jeffrey was about five feet tall and was one of the new DTR series of robots. Jeffrey had the new i7 processor in his brain, which made him about twice as intelligent as previous robots. He had the new 975bxt3 printer in his body, which was able to print out just about any newspaper, from anywhere in the world, and with impressive speeds.

"What newspaper would you like, sir?"

"Um, give me the local one please."

"The Megaton Sun or The State, sir?"

"The Megaton Sun."

"Yes, sir."

Immediately, Jeffrey started to print out the newspaper. In about ten seconds, the printing had finished. He made a beeping sound to let Vlad know the printing was complete. Jeffrey's mouth opened. The newspaper slowly ejected out. He reached into his mouth and placed the paper on the island, next to Vlad.

"Here you go, sir. I've placed the Sports section on top, 'cause I know it's your favourite."

"Thank-you, Jeffrey."

Jeffrey then entered power saving mode. His hands lowered to his sides and he began self charging.

Vlad opened the newspaper, and it made a crinkling sound as he flipped to the first page. The pages were still warm from the printing process. The headline read,

"The Altec Fighters beat the Lansing Grizzly's, 10-8"

"Oh, that's good," Vlad said to himself. Vlad liked the sport of fighting. He would always watch it with his father when he was just a wee lad. Now that his father had passed away, he would usually watch fighting on his television with Jeffrey. His father would place his arm around his neck and hold him. It just wasn't the same when Jeffrey did it.

There was a knock at the door. Jeffrey exited from power saving mode.

"Sir, your milk and eggs have arrived. Shall I go get them?"

"Nah, I'll get 'em Jeffrey."

Vlad placed his mug on the table. He slid out from underneath the table and walked towards the door. He looked at the monitor located on the door. He could see the FedEx delivery robot. Vlad unlocked the door and swung it open.

"Package for Vlad. Please swipe your finger over the scanner on my face to confirm your identity."

Vlad swiped his finger over the scanner. The words "Identifying..." appeared on the robot's facial monitor. A beeping sound confirmed his identity.

"Thank-you, Mr. Vlad. Here is your package. Would you care to give me a tip for my visit today?"

Vlad really had no choice. FedEx robots tended to stick around until you gave them some sort of reward for their visit. He reached into his pocket and pulled out a dollar. A change slot opened on the top of the robot's head. He slid the coin in.

"Thank-you. Have a nice day, sir."

"Shut up."

The FedEx robot turned around and walked down the steps from his home. Vlad closed the door and walked the package over to the island. He sat on his stool.

"Scissors please, Jeffrey."

"Yes, sir."

Jeffrey opened the compartment in his stomach. An error message appeared on his monitor.

"Sir, I don't have any scissors in my system. Let me scan your residence for them. One moment please."

The words *"Scissors found!"* appeared on Jeffrey's monitor.

"It appears your scissors are located in your office. Allow me to go and retrieve them."

Vlad picked up his coffee mug and lifted it to his lips. He then slowly took a sip. It was hot. A moment later, Jeffrey appeared from around the corner. He rolled into the kitchen, holding the scissors in his hand. He handed them to Vlad.

"There you are, sir."

"Thank-you, Jeffrey."

Vlad cut open the package. He was greeted with a FedEx thank you card. He threw the card on the floor. Jeffrey rolled up to the card and took it to the trash can. Vlad took out a dozen eggs and the two jugs of milk. He placed them on the table.

"Jeffrey, wanna put these in the fridge for me?"

"But of course, sir."

Jeffrey picked up the package off the table. He rolled over and opened the fridge with one hand, while holding the goods in the other. He placed them in, and closed it shut.

"There you are, sir."

Vlad said nothing. He picked up the newspaper and continued to read. He flipped over the page to the *"buy and sell"* section.

"Hey Jeffrey, check this out."

Jeffrey rolled over to Vlad. He was pointing at an ad for an older version of a home robot. The robot was from the much older SRT series. These robots tended to crash into walls every time someone was on the phone within 200 metres of them. The signals from the phone would interfere with the robots wireless signals and make them do strange things besides crashing into walls.

"I can't believe these things are still around. My dad had one when I was about five years old."

"Sir, my on board computer tells me you have work in 20 minutes. Shall I send Oscar2 down here to get you ready?"

"Oh, that's right. I have a presentation with the senior partners today. Yes, send down Oscar2 immediately."

Three consecutive beeps came from Jeffrey's built in speaker. These beeps paged Oscar2 to let him know he was needed in the kitchen.

Oscar2 was a slim robot, with a rounded over head. He had four arms which helped humans get ready for just about every occasion. He had a deep, Russian sounding voice which sometimes frightened Vlad. Oscar2 appeared from the Travel Tube. He slid out from the chamber and rolled towards Jeffrey and Vlad.

"Oscar2, at your service."

"Yes Oscar2, get me ready for work please."

"Yes sir. Please select the suit in which you would like to be dressed in today."

A touch screen monitor slid out from Oscar2's mouth. Vlad

scrolled through the options.

"Hey! Where's my favourite blue tie?"

"Sir, it is at the dry cleaners. You spilt coffee on it on Thursday."

"Oh yeah...Okay, I guess I will go with the red tie today."

"Sir, please press "OK" to confirm your option."

Vlad pressed "OK". Oscar2 approached him. His stomach doors opened, and one of his arms reached in and pulled out the suit that Vlad had chosen. With his other arm he undressed Vlad from his pyjamas and pulled out a toothbrush.

"What flavour toothpaste would you like, sir?"

"Vanilla."

Oscar2 squeezed some vanilla paste on the toothbrush. He opened up Vlad's mouth with his other hand and gave him a good scrub. He then placed the toothbrush back into his body. Oscar2 pulled out a tiny hose and rinsed Vlad's mouth out. He placed the hose back in and pulled out a little plastic cup.

"Spit, sir."

Vlad spat into the cup. Oscar2 placed the spit cup back into his body. He then pulled out a comb and combed his hair. He then grabbed a pair of boxers from his body and slid them onto Vlad's body. Oscar2 put the suit onto Vlad.

"There you are, sir. I must say you look great this morning."

"All thanks to you Oscar2."

"Thank-you, sir."

"Well, I'm off to work. Jeffrey, if you could be so kind as to give the place a light dusting while I'm gone."

"But of course, sir"

"Thank-you, Jeffrey."

Vlad walked towards the door. Jeffrey rolled over to Vlad and held out his arm. He sat on his arm and put on his shoes. He stood up and grabbed his briefcase and walked out the door. Vlad slid his finger over the door lock, closing it.

"Activate Alarm."

From the intercom he heard "Alarm Activated." Vlad walked down his driveway. He swiped his finger over his vintage 1967 Corvette convertible. As he bent over to place the briefcase in his car, he stepped in and the door slowly closed behind him.

"Hello, Vlad. You look stupendous today. Where shall I take you?"

"To the office, please."

"Absolutely. Would you like to listen to some music while you wait?"

"Yeah, maybe some soothing jazz."

"Yes sir."

The seatbelt came from behind his shoulder and locked in. The radio came on and the car was filled with the relaxing music of Kenny G. Vlad reached for the lever and reclined the chair back and closed his eyes.

Outside, all was calm. It had just snowed yesterday and there was about two inches of it on the ground. There were humans and robots walking on the sidewalk. Children were running to school with packs on their backs. They also had miniature guide robots hovering right behind them, following their every move and guiding them to their destination. To the right of the vehicle, you could see "*Shop-O-Rama*," a giant mall that was about 20 million square-feet in size. You were able to see humans moving around on hover boards and stopping at shop entrances to browse goods. Just about everything you could possibly imagine could be bought at "*Shop-O-Rama*." The mall was divided up by countries. Each country bought a section of the mall to house their goods. Whatever that country made was sold in their section of the store.

After passing the mall, a needle shape building was seen in the distance; Vlad's office. By going mach 2, the trip to the office had taken about five minutes, and that was in heavy traffic. The car suddenly came to a stop in front of Vlad's workplace.

"You have arrived at your destination."

Vlad reached for the lever and slid the chair back into the upright position. The door opened slowly. Vlad unbuckled his seatbelt, picked up his briefcase and stepped out of his car. Outside, the street life was booming. There were people walking past each other on sidewalks, stopping to greet each other with their morning nutrition drinks in their hands. These nutrition drinks had everything the doctor recommends daily for fruits, vegetables, meat, dairy and grain products.

Vlad stepped towards the entrance to the needle shaped building. A Greeter Robot opened the door for him. He stepped through the doorway and walked past the reception desk. Wanda, a quite chubby lady, greeted him.

"Hello, Vlad. How are we today?"

"Quite well Wanda. Thanks for asking."

Vlad approached the elevator and stepped onto the platform and a protective cage came down from above him and locked shut. A robot greeted him in an electronic voice.

"Hello, Vlad. What floor?"

"Twenty-Seven."

"Right away, sir."

A moment later, the elevator stopped. The cage shot up to the roof and Vlad stepped into his office. The floor made a squeak as he walked over the dark hardwood floors. He walked over to the fireplace and took off his shoes. Vlad bent down and put them side by side neatly. As he walked over to the desk, he placed the briefcase on it and took a seat in a high back leather chair. Vlad breathed in deeply, and then exhaled.

"It's time."

He opened the briefcase, and pushed the trigger. The E.M.P. pulse raced across the town, destroying every electrical device in its path. The lights had suddenly burned out. Hot glass shattered and fell on top of Vlad's head. The room was dark, except for the fireplace in the corner. Screams from men, women and children filled the streets below. Scrap metal from cars were now scattered across the highway. Pools of blood from accidents flowed to the sewer drains.

The fireplace was shining and flickering on Vlad's face. He grinned. Vlad got up and closed the briefcase.

"Let's see how they recover from this one..."

FINDING AIDEN
JORDAN KARRYS

MY feet led me on, one after the other, trudging through the hot sand, stumbling all the while. Even though I was still dazed from the previous encounter, I was aware of the sound of the other hostages trudging along behind me. We were being led somewhere but I didn't know where because I could not see. The blindfold did its job well. Suddenly, I could feel the heat of the sun sliding off my shoulders. We were somewhere shaded and cool. I had no idea where we were, but it had to be miles from the domes. Our blindfolds were roughly removed. I glanced around, as my eyes adjusted, and saw that we were in a cave. A woman's loud, controlling voice cut the silence and echoed off the cave walls. She stood in front of us and stated, "You are now rebels. Life here will be hard for you, but you have no choice. If you want to leave, you can go, but good luck finding another shithole to suck away your brains." Every word she spoke flamed with a passion I had never heard before. She raised her chin and continued, "My name is Ember. Half of you will be coming with me and I will be giving you tasks to help everyone survive in our society". She paced in front of us, and paused as she stared into the face of one of the other men, then she continued to speak loudly and clearly, "The other half will go with Darius. Darius, like me, is one of the leaders of the rebel groups. He and I lead this group together. He has a great deal of knowledge about life as a rebel and can teach you a lot. Darius will lead you to a neighbouring rebel society." After a long, deep breath she looked up wistfully and said "Soon, hopefully very soon, we will be going on a long journey to a place that outshines the domes with a true glory. A place where we can live from the land." A small smile spread on her face and she once again looked at us, loud enough for everything around for miles to hear, she shouted, "Your life begins now!" The other rebels cheered excitedly, but I did not.

We were instructed to rest for a brief period, and as I

slumped down to the ground, I looked around. I recognized many of the other hostages. They were from the same dome as me. For some reason, this made me feel very anti-social. Thoughts started to fill my mind, blocking out all sounds until only white noise filled my head. I don't know how long I had sat, but I was suddenly snapped back to reality by the sound of Ember's voice.

"You, what is your name?" Her tone seemed very impatient.

"Ai- Ai- Aiden", I stuttered in reply.

"Well Aiden, you're with me. I know this is all confusing, but it will get easier with time, I promise."

Her voice was calm now and she was speaking directly to me, something I had not experienced before. I felt strange inside, and was having feelings I had never felt before. Ember looked into my face and continued as she held her hand out to me. I grasped hold of her long fingers and struggled to my feet. "Aiden" she said, "Our life as rebels is not so simple." We were walking now and she was guiding me around the cave as she continued to speak, "But we would not survive if the rebel community didn't work as one." The tour of the cave was brief and it soon ended and even though I had listened to everything Ember had said, I still felt as though I had missed some of what she was telling me. It was so hard to concentrate on what she was saying because I was struggling to understand the feelings inside me. Every time I looked into her face, her black hair fell forward creating an aura of mystery. It didn't completely cover her face, and I could still see her piercing, emerald green eyes. Her eyes made me feel things I did not understand. I felt like I had butterflies fluttering around in my stomach. Ember was unlike any woman I had ever seen. Her body looked strong and healthy. Her clothes were made from leather that showed her shape, and she wore rugged boots that fit the shape of her legs. Such clothes were not worn by the women in the dome; they all dressed like the men. It suddenly occurred to me that everyone in the dome wore the same clothes and that they resembled a uniform. We all dressed in white pants and loose fitting white tops. Everything we wore hung loosely, disguising the shape of the body, and from a distance everyone looked the same. The only skin visible was on our arms, as the shirts were short sleeved. Ember's clothes, however, showed a lot of skin, and it appeared to be darkened by the sun, giving her a brown glow. I must have been staring at her as she suddenly barked, "Aiden, pay attention." I shook my head as she went on, "we must all help one another in order for everyone to survive." Our tour had reached the back of the cave and Ember stopped in front of a man. "Aiden this is Darius," she looked at him then me and said, "It will be your job to help Darius carry water to other rebel communities. This is important, as not all our settlements can easily find water." My jaw dropped, "I thought I was going to be with you" again I was stuttering. Why did words escape me when I looked at her? Ember laughed, "We'll see how you do with this first." She reached up to pat my shoulder and her touch made my heart pound. I felt suddenly confused. How could this be happening? Everything in the dome was so controlled by the main computers. Schedules were given to each inhabitant and jobs were assigned by the computers. The day began and ended at the same times. Even the atmosphere was carefully controlled by the computers. As a society, the people within the domes didn't have to think at all, as all the thinking was done for us. Life had become one of service. We served to make life in the dome comfortable for everyone, and we seldom thought of ourselves. It was a fairly simple life and I never thought that there was any other way to live. That was until now, as I stood in the rebel cave looking into the face of this brave and outspoken woman. I realized that by living in the dome I had become somewhat mindless, never thinking about what I was doing. I, and everyone else in the domes, had lost touch with what it was like to be a free thinker. I don't ever remember having any feelings like this before. Ember quickly pointed to a jug and stated, "This one is yours." Darius quickly took command. He smirked then said, "I shall lead the way."

My knees wobbled as I attempted to pick up the jug. I looked at the others in the group, and seeing that I was the only one having trouble, I blushed. I felt dizzy but tried again, and on the second try, I lifted the jug. I watched Darius lift his jug to his shoulder and struggled to copy him. It felt strange, but after a minute or so, it felt better. Darius walked and I followed. My knees kept wobbling a little, but I kept going. We exited the cave and the sun was right overhead. Darius bellowed, "We have a five mile walk ahead of us, so keep up." We had hardly begun and already Darius was far ahead of us, continuing without looking back. I had never exerted myself so much in all my life. I followed Darius and marveled at his strength. He made the job look easy. I could see the muscles of his back flex as he walked. He was tall and lean, with tanned dark hair and tanned skin. The water didn't seem to be heavy for him. I found it very heavy, and I was tired. I concentrated on following Darius' footprints in the sand. With every step, it became harder and all I could think of doing was ripping open the water jug and drowning myself in the clear, cool water. Not knowing how far we had gone, or how far was left to go, I could not help but to drag my feet and trudge on. I know the others were dragging their feet too. The sun was dropping down below the horizon, and I wondered if we would walk forever. Suddenly I could hear laughter and whistling ahead. I looked up and squinted. I could see caves and a group of people gathered around a fire. As we approached the group, a large man joked, "Well pull up a seat". He put his arm around Darius' shoulders and laughed. Darius began to laugh too. They looked as though they would fall over from laughing so hard. I didn't understand what was so funny and I rolled my eyes up. It was then I realized night had fallen, and I saw the sky for the first time. It was sprinkled with shining white stars.

"Beautiful, isn't it?" Darius said with a smile.

"Yes" I answered, baffled. "Is this what living is like?"

"No, this is just surviving" he answered. Then just as the last person from our group stepped into the cave, Darius started to leave and called to us, "Now we walk back." For some reason I felt a need to prove myself to this strange man, Darius, and I tried to keep pace with him. After some time I looked behind me to see how many were in our group. We began as twelve but now I could only see five.

"Half of them are gone" I said, panicked.

"Those ones are weak. Leave them" Darius replied sternly.

I couldn't believe what I had just heard. "No, I won't!" I stated. Darius stopped and turned on me. "You will leave them, or you will be one of them." I shook my head as he continued, "You don't seem to understand that out here life is different. The strong survive, and they don't let the weak drag them down." He sighed, and then said, "It may seem hard and cruel, but it is the only way. If we don't stay strong we all die, and then what good have we had done?" I didn't know what to say, so I just listened.

"You have lived your whole life in a controlled dome. You have been taught how to feel, or really how not to feel. You have had everything controlled for you. No decisions were ever made by you. Everything you did was for the 'collective'; or the dome. Never did you do any thinking for yourself."

I didn't want to believe him, but I knew it was true. The computers in the dome had controlled everything and everybody. From as far back as I could remember it had been that way, never once had I made a decision for myself. I didn't know if I could do it. Darius watched me. I struggled with myself. What should I do? Was he right? Do only the strong survive? I realized that I had to make a decision for myself, but I didn't know what was right. Should I save myself and let the others die? Didn't Ember tell me that we have to help each other to survive? It was so confusing as now the other rebel leader was telling me that only the strong survive and the weak should be left behind. Suddenly it came to me, that I did have the power to decide. I decided to help those that I could, and I turned back. I was sure that Darius would leave me to die also. With every step I took away from him my heart pounded louder and faster, and a cold feeling spread through my veins. I had never experienced so many different emotions in one day and it was a little overwhelming.

As I continued to walk and put distance between Darius and myself, it dawned on me that I didn't really know what I was doing. I thought about things for a moment and decided that the people left behind would be scattered. How would I gather them all up? I decided that I would go first to the one furthest behind the group. After deciding my course of action, I felt a need to move faster and I started to jog. I passed some who had fallen and I told them to wait and I would be back for them. Finally I reached the person I believed to be the last of the group. It was a woman. She lay so still that I was afraid she was dead. I could hardly tell she was breathing, until I put my face close to hers and I felt short weak breaths against my cheek. I reached under her body to pick her up. She wasn't heavy and she seemed so frail. I realized everyone from the domes was frail. I started to walk back, retracing my steps. The wind blew against us and bounced off her body, into my face. I stumbled and she opened her eyes to look up into my face. Her eyes were a pale blue, a colour that reminded me of how thirsty I was. I wanted to stop, but she looked at me and I knew she was depending on me to help her. I stared blankly ahead of me. I felt her body tense in my arms and she began to speak in a panicked tone. "What's going on?" I could feel her heartbeat quicken until it was pounding so hard, I was sure her heart would burst out of her chest. "I'm taking you back,"

I said, without looking at her. I surprised myself. My voice was calm, yet commanding. I was in control, something I had never experienced before. She seemed to think for a moment, and then she wrapped her arm around me and quietly said, "Thank you."

The wind pelted us and it became hard to see. The journey back seemed to be taking longer than it should. I felt like we were perhaps wandering in circles and a hopeless feeling washed over me. The woman in my arms seemed heavier with every passing second. Suddenly I faltered and fell forward. I managed to roll to the side, so the woman landed on top of me. Every muscle in my body screamed. "Help" I moaned, "Somebody help us". My pleas were drowned out by the wind and blowing sand. I felt the weight of the woman on my chest and it was hard to breathe. All we could do was wait. We waited for what felt like hours, until I felt movement by my arm. The sand was moving and I looked up into a face I had seen before. There, peering down at me, were those piercing, emerald eyes.

"Ember, the others, we have to find the others."

My yells were heard as though they were whispers in the wind. "My rebel scouts are ahead of me and sent word that they found the others," she yelled back, and I could see a wide smile brighten her face. I felt someone lift the woman off of my chest and then hands grabbed me and helped me up. I must have fallen asleep, because when I awoke, I was no longer in the wind and sand. I was lying on a bed made of thick straw, in a room with an opening covered by green curtains. I was confused and I couldn't exactly remember what had happened. I remembered a woman and felt a sudden fear wash over me. Had I left her in the desert? I felt something new, perhaps guilt and sorrow. I climbed out of the straw bed. My muscles were stiff. I reached up and pushed aside the curtains. There on the other side of the opening sat Ember. I looked down at her. She must have seen my concern as she softly smiled and said, "It's okay, we got them all." Then her expression changed and she clenched her teeth, "Darius was a fool to leave you like that." She sighed and stood up.

"I have to go as it is late."

"Why? Where are you going?" I tried to conceal the concern without success.

"It's okay Aiden, we won't be gone long"

"We? Who else is going with you?"

Ember smiled "A group of rebels are going to free more hostages from the domes."

"I want to come" I said, as I walked out of the curtained exit.

"You'll stay." Ember's tone was hard but softened as she added. "You have had a long day."

I wasn't going to take no for an answer and I walked forward declaring, "No. I am coming." Ember must have known from the tone of my voice that I had made my mind up, so she sighed and declared, "Then you stay with me."

The group of rebels including myself, numbered at twelve. We had made our way quietly toward the dome. Everything seemed quiet and there didn't seem to be anybody around. The dome suddenly disappeared from view as a strange wind picking up the sand, created a wall around it. Ember and the other leaders of the group, including Darius, seemed surprised by the appearance of the wind. "This is odd" said Ember. Her statement was met with a short laugh from Darius. "Everything about the domes is odd" he added sarcastically. Ember shot him a look of anger and he stopped talking. It seemed as though the group of rebels didn't know what to do with the unexpected wind. I stood listening to them discuss and bicker about what to do. I held in my hand a rope that we had brought with us. I could see the wind coming closer to the group and realized that soon we would be shrouded by the sand that it was stirring up. I dropped one end of the rope and tied the other around my waist. Suddenly I was yelling at the group to do the same.

"Tie yourselves to one another."

Darius was not used to taking orders from others, and it was clear by the look on his face that he didn't like me telling him what to do. He stood still for a moment. Ember, however, picked up the rope and tied it around her waist as she yelled, "As I said, you stay with me." It wasn't long before everyone was tied to a rope. Each rope was joined at the ends so that we formed a human chain. This way we had less chance of losing one another in the blinding sand storm. I wasn't sure of the plan, except that we were going to enter the dome through an escape hatch in one of the lower panels. We worked as a group to reach the hatch. It was a struggle but we managed to find our way. Once inside the dome the wind and sand stopped blowing. Everything was quiet. In fact it was too quiet. Even while living in the dome I had never known it be so quiet. I felt the hair on the back of my neck prickle and started to speak, "I don't think everything…" I was suddenly interrupted by the sound of screaming people. There was a sudden loud noise and I felt panic rise inside me. "What the hell is that?" Ember shouted. I felt sick but managed to yell back, "it's the alarm that tells everyone in the dome that their lives are in danger." People poured out of every building. They ran toward us screaming in what seemed to be angry voices. I found this confusing, as never, while living in the dome, had I known anyone to be angry, or to yell. A look of shock registered on the faces of the others in the group. "They look like an angry mob of puppets" Darius yelled above the loud screams. "It's the computers," Ember shouted, "They are controlling the people by sounding the alarm." I had never realized this before, but deep down I knew she was right. The computers had controlled every aspect of life, from the weather and the lives of the people. I surprised myself as I yelled "We have to stop them." Darius had already untied his rope and was running toward the wall of the dome. Each dome contained ladders that allowed a person to climb up to a platform that circled the uppermost part. He was quickly and smoothly climbing the ladder. Close on his heels were many of the dome people. They were definitely trying to stop him from reaching the top of the dome, as it is, at the top, that the computer controlling the dome is found.

While Darius climbed the rest of the group tried to distract the angry mob. We screamed and threw rocks and other debris we were able to find, at the people. It worked a little as many of the people were once again coming toward us. I looked around and recognized many of the faces, even though they had a blank expression, but they clearly didn't recognize me. The plan was working, and we were managing to keep enough of the people from noticing what Darius was doing and he had almost reached the computer panel in the center of the dome. I was so interested in what Darius was doing that I didn't notice Ember was being overtaken by many from the mob of angry people. They had rushed toward her and grabbed her, lifting her into the air. I looked over to her in horror and ran to help her. I found a new strength in me and I started to push and strike the people holding Ember. Many seemed surprised at my attacks. It was such a surprise that it caused them to stop completely. I yelled at the rebel group, many of whom were hiding from the dome people, "Attack them. They don't know how to respond to aggression. "Many of the rebels took my advice and ran at the mob. It worked as the dome people all stopped and looked around confused. Our actions again worked and it gave Darius enough time to get to the computer panel. Without too much trouble he managed to open the panel and start cutting wires. The alarm stopped sounding and I smiled, thinking it was all over. Unfortunately I was premature in my happy thought, as suddenly there was a loud crack of thunder, and the sky in the dome was lit by lightening. Almost immediately a heavy rain began to fall and a stiff wind started to howl. The people from the dome rushed for cover. Some made it into the buildings, but others were stuck, exposed to the extreme weather conditions caused by the computer. I grabbed Ember and dragged her behind a huge rock. We were both soaked to the skin. The wind got faster and it felt as though it would rip our skin from our bodies. I closed my eyes and held onto Ember, praying in my head that Darius would succeed in disabling the computer completely. It was as though my prayers were answered, when suddenly the wind subsided and the thunder stopped. I opened my eyes and looked around. Ember looked at me as she slowly crawled from our hiding spot. I followed her. The people of the dome were exiting the buildings. They looked a little lost and unsure.

"Where are we?" one of the women from the dome asked.

"You are free," I answered.

Darius climbed down to join the rebels once more.

"Well," he said with a smile, "It seems we have many more to join our group."

Seeing as the computer had stopped functioning all the people in the dome were able to do whatever they pleased. They all seemed confused, but happy. A great gathering happened in the center of the dome and the rebels told the dome people what had happened to them. They explained that many years ago the domes were built to protect man from a hostile environment. At first the computers were supposed to help the people living in the domes. However, as time went on the computers became more and more powerful. They began to take over. They not only controlled the weather and when the day began and ended, they also began to control the people. The computers started to think for those in the dome, until eventually the computers were completely controlling the people, including their thoughts and feelings. The rebels had realized what was going on and had decided it was time to save the people. This was why the rebels raided the domes to take people. They were not taking hostages, even though that is what the dome people thought was happening. The rebels had freed the people that they considered hostages within the domes. The rebels felt that the computers were going to continue to take over until everything that man had ever known before the domes, was completely gone. The dome people sat and listened. Many looked like they had just woken up from a long dream. Others looked like they had been thinking the same way as the rebels for a while. These people looked very happy to be saved from the computers.

All of the domes were eventually destroyed by the very people living in them. After the destruction of the domes, the barren landscape found on the outside of the dome walls changed. Once again plants and grass grew. It was after then, that the people realized just how much the computers had controlled. Somehow they had manipulated the environment outside of the dome making it barren and uninhabitable. This way, the people thought they had no choice but to live inside the domes. It was not until the rebels started to rescue people, did the truth start to surface and a different future become possible for everyone. Many stories were told about the computers that controlled man. The rebels led the people to the land of green fields and flowing water, and surprisingly it was found not too far from the domes. It seems that the computers had made the environment outside the domes hostile so over time, the landscape became one of green hills and softly blowing wind, where the people could live off the land, and where anyone could say what they wanted and live in any way they desired.

FINE MARGINS
ROSS ARMOUR

AS the alarm clock sounded, Dr. Neville Stanley Bartham sat up, stepped out of his bed and opened the curtains. There were a few clouds in the sky, with the sun attempting to break through; in order to show off its majestic presence. A ray of light came through Neville's flat window and rebounded off the mirror, into his eyes. Dr. Bartham shielded them quickly. This ray of light was to symbolize things to come. A ray of hope. But whether this hope was to end in joy, it remained to be unseen.

It was about 5 degrees in downtown, New York City, quite cold for August. Dr. Bartham closed his flat door and set off on another remarkable adventure to his laboratory across the street. Dressed in his usual knee-length, white lab coat, Bartham was easily spotted from afar. His daily schedule lasted for approximately 14 hours, between 6:05 AM to 8:05 PM. During this period, Bartham spent his time researching into the fine art of chemistry. In an attempt to find a life-saving cure for the most inhospitable illnesses, such as cancer and heart disease. Occasionally, he would be spotted by pedestrians leaving his lab at around noon, supposedly to grab something to eat. Nicknamed "The Good Doctor", Bartham was seen by most as a warm-hearted and modest man, who took pride in his work. He was also greatly respected, mainly due to his desire to help the community and the world.

In the previous year, the number of cancer deaths reached a peak. As a result, the start of the current year, urged him to set a two year target of finding either a new substance, or machine that would enable these illnesses to be cured. It was a task of which no man had previously succeeded in doing. In a public speech at Central Park; an action that Dr. Bartham often carried out, he was quoted in saying; "My goal is to find the power within nature to cure this most dreadful situation. I plan to achieve this goal with flying colours. The completion should be arriving within the next two years."

Often, throughout his career in chemistry, Bartham would suffer from criticism and acts of jealousy. Fortunately, for his own self esteem, he was able to realize that this would come naturally. After achieving his degree, at a pass rate of 98% at Yale University, some of Bartham's fellow colleagues commented on him in a negative manner. The fact that he had made such an easy job out of one of the hardest courses available frustrated a few. That only made The Good Doctor more determined and mentally strong in life. With it, came an heir of confidence that he placed into every aspect of this phenomenal man's work, to date.

***

Today was August the 12th. It was the first day of the "Two Year Plan". By the time he left work, it was around 6:22 AM, a late night. Bartham logged on to his trademark Mac computer, which was obviously the best in the business. He searched the World Wide Web for at least a couple of hours; the only body movement he carried out was to move the mouse. He was acting in the most serious of ways than he had ever acted before. Within that period of time, Bartham had gathered some information on the micro-organisms contained within cancer. He managed to find out the fact to why the tiny bacteria within the illness, were resistant to the element Boron. This particular element was one that was very rarely found in nature. Also, it was stated that the bacteria were only resistant to it, if the Boron was in liquid-form. Bartham realized that he could easily get Boron to react with Hydrogen in order to create Boronic Acid, a liquidized substance. It would be attempting to get a hold of the element that would be the difficult thing.

Between 8:00 AM and 12:00 PM, the doctor began writing some notes regarding the formula of Boronic Acid. This was a skill within chemistry that came naturally to him. The process would be carried out on his chalkboard. Bartham produced an equation that was balanced enough to carry out the reaction between Hydrogen and Boron. The research and brain bursts continued throughout the day.

As he lay in bed that night, Dr. Bartham realized that one part of his quest to find the cure for cancer had been completed. It's a shame this part only counted for about a tenth! He knew he needed to find some extracts of Boron in the near future. But how?

That night, Neville dreamed of seeing himself on T.V. He was set to become a billionaire after the biggest breakthrough in world history. His face was broadcasted

nationally, and he was now the most popular human being walking on planet Earth.

Suddenly... The alarm clock sounded. Another hard-hitting day of work lay ahead. Number 2 of 730.

***

Four months later, December 14th at about 3:43 PM, the telephone at the rear of the laboratory started ringing. It was a unique sort of ring, one of determination. Bartham felt confused. Nobody ever phoned him. They wouldn't dare interrupt him from his work, would they? The doctor turned his head in the direction of the phone. At the same time he felt a rampant creaking sound, seemingly coming from his neck muscles, like an old man turning to reach his newspaper. Bartham was only 28 years old.

He stood up, walked towards the phone, and picked it up. The dust flew into

his eyes. "Hello," he said in a deep, American accent that he'd inherited. There was

silence for 5 seconds, as a sense of caution and fear filled Bartham's gut. The awkward

feeling was relieved soon after, as a voice replied from the other end of the line with a

sound of enthusiasm.

"Hi there! My name is Marc Speight. I'm calling from Auckland, New Zealand. I

received details of your situation from my friend in Manhattan regarding your cure for

cancer drive. Would you care to explain in more detail?"

The caution and fear had vanished, but the confusion still remained within the

mind of Bartham. Why was this one man, from a million miles away, so keen on knowing his business? After a few moments Bartham answered, "Well... Err; yes I'm trying to find a cure for cancer. Why do you query?"

"My friend tells me you require an extract of the element Boron to continue your study."

"That is correct."

"Well I believe I may be able to help you with that."

Bartham's eyes lit up like Christmas lights. The idea of victory suddenly became

present.

"Do you, um, Marc. Do you carry some of the Boron element?"

"I do indeed. A couple of decades back I owned this piece of land that contained

thousands of gallons of crude oil beneath its surface. I was fortunate enough to extract a

portion of the oil. Now, obviously it contained a lot of impurities and I believe one of

these to be the element Boron."

"Is there any way you could send me a portion?"

"No problem. I'll get it to ya ASAP!"

"Thank you so much. I can't describe how much this means to me."

Bartham couldn't believe his luck. After a few months of constant struggle, a major stumbling block was about to be conquered. He felt an amazing sense of satisfaction that no words could describe. It was like a soldier had just defeated an enemy trench line, and moved forward a hundred metres into the next stage of battle.

***

It was on February 9th that the inevitable arrived. Packaged inside a dark ivory
box, was what felt like a ton of Boron. Bartham stored it under one of his radioactive calming machines. The rest of the day was spent creating the acid. It was the type of reaction that didn't always happen first time round. After attempt number five, the recipe finally came together. The Boronic Acid had been created. All that was left to do, was put it into action.

After years of scientific research, Bartham knew that the chemical Boron was too dangerous to be extracted by hand. It was now the job of, The Good Doctor, to create a machine similar to the mechanism a doctor uses on cancer patients. At that point, Neville Stanley Bartham's ultimate dream, would become reality.

***

The rest of spring and early summer was a difficult period. However, it was one that would result in the most beneficial achievements. Bartham spent the season in his engineering department, accompanied at times by his cousin, who was an engineer. The daily papers were flooded with excitement. Headlines included: "Cure for Cancer, Soon To Be Here"; "Our Bodies' Greatest Killer Will Soon Meet It's Match"; "The True End of Cancer" and "A Man Destined For Glory." The latter obviously referred to Bartham and his work.

All in all, it took five long, aggravating and painful months to create a piece of technology that was soon to make history. Nicknamed "Bartham's Blaster", this machine weighed around 120 pounds. It was made of steel and was covered in a coat of white paint. This particular colour symbolised purity and innocence. Bartham allowed his creation to first be paraded on Independence Day in New York City, so the world could witness the machine. Within these months, Bartham had devised the exact formula in which the acid could be inserted within, and then placed inside a patient's system.

A couple of days after the parade, an email came through on Bartham's computer, inviting him to put his work to the test on a patient in Queensland, Australia. The patient's name was Sophie Bennett, a name that Bartham had never come across. Not that it bothered him. He was a man who believed in equality for all and attempted to save anyone's life that was displayed before him.

Bartham booked a flight for July 15th. The operation was due to take place on the 20th. Once again, another sense came into Bartham's mind. This time it was one of shear disbelief. This "Two Year Plan," that was broadcasted so long ago, would all come together over a year ahead of scheduled intent.

The acid, and everything else involved, flew out on the same day as Bartham. An audience of thousands gathered inside JFK airport, including the media, in hope of seeing

him fly out, and achieve his desired goal. The most famous headline on this day was "The Flight to Heaven." All the other headlines were derived around this idea.

Once his plane touched down at the airport, Bartham and his "tools" were driven to Rosebud General Hospital. As he entered, the mode of tension was felt instantly. Bartham slammed the door shut with ferocious intensity as he was determined for all of this to happen quickly. The noise created by the door, alarmed all those inside the hospital's reception room. At that point, a mass of people swarmed upon Bartham like bees in a honey pot. Most attempted to shake his hand, but only some succeeded. Bartham was perceived as Jesus in disguise. It was indeed as if the Lord's greatest gift had arrived in their eyes.

Eventually, Bartham weaved pass the crowd and immediately rushed down the corridor, towards the theatre room. His machine and the acid were stored within that particular area of the hospital. He spent the day meeting the doctor and nurses he'd be working with and the patient herself. She had blonde hair and was very polite and glamorous. She was the type of girl all men dreamed of dating. Bartham was put up in a five star hotel, just a couple of minutes walking distance from the hospital. A long, uncomfortable, sleepless night lied ahead.

The next day, Bartham took up his position in the theatre at around 8:30 AM. Sophie Bennett was brought in at 9:03 AM. She was suffering from breast cancer, one of the most common types of cancer. The operation began at 9:14 AM. Bartham measured out exactly 15.1 millilitres of Boronic Acid on a measuring device that was present on the blaster. Bartham had already calculated that anything more or less than 15.1 ml would cause the entire procedure to fail. The fine margins that were present, could not be more precise, could they?

The rest was left to the doctor and nurses.

Fourteen long hours passed by, and Bartham patiently waited outside the theatre. He sat still, with a feeling of terror and optimism. He wanted this to be a success so badly but at the same time, a girl's life was to be saved.

Another half hour passed and a man came down the corridor. Running fast in an
anxious manner.

"How is she?" he cried.

"No word yet. Who are you?" replied Bartham in question.

"I am Sophie's father. My name is Marc."

Before Bartham could reply, an aspect of déjà vu came into play. Could this be the man that got him here today.....?

"I am Marc Speight. The man who supplied you with the Boron."

It *was* him, Bartham couldn't believe his eyes. It was as if the Holy Spirit stood before him. Without thinking, Bartham leapt up off the bench and hugged Marc. This whole event had now become the most important event that Bartham had ever been involved in.

Suddenly, a door cranked open. It was the door to the theatre, a nurse stood before the two men. She looked worried, but neutral. The eyes of the two men widened an extra inch or two. Bartham's whole career was about to be either plunged into darkness, or lit up with victory. He tried to think positive, and had never felt more nervous. Marc was first to speak. "Well........?"

The nurse answered quickly. "Mr Speight, unfortunately your daughter passed
away around five minutes ago."

Defeat was felt throughout all involved. Marc began to cry and weep as if being
tortured and humiliated. Bartham's head flopped down. He knew he had failed.

"I'm afraid Sophie's body didn't take to the Boronic Acid. Instead, it only catalyzed her inevitable death."

"But, why?" queried Bartham. "Everything was in place."

"It is believed that too much Boronic Acid was inserted into the patient's system."

"But, but, I inputted the correct amount, didn't I?"

"You thought you did."

Bartham felt as though the nurse was publicly cursing him. "Sadly, you accidentally inserted 0.001 millilitres too much. I am so sorry Mr. Speight."

By this time, Marc had vanished from the room. Bartham did not see where he had gone. The nurse returned inside the theatre. The feeling inside Bartham's mind was now one of deep frustration and sadness. It was supposed to be victorious and joyful. Bartham didn't even get a chance to apologise to the man, who so nearly made him famous.

An hour and a quarter passed before Bartham returned to his hotel room. He was due to fly back to America the following day. The difference of a thousandth of a millilitre was the difference between fame and failure, life and death.

It was later broadcasted nationally that Dr. Neville Stanley Bartham never returned to New York City after that night. Instead, he was found a few days later, by the cleaner, hanging helplessly from the wooden ceiling, a rope around his neck. His failure had driven this man far enough, to take his own life.

Bartham's heart, brain, mind, and soul had never experienced failure before.

He had always been victorious. Unfortunately, the fine margins had proven to be too strong and influential for this, once called, "Great Man" to continue in life again.

He was later buried in Death Valley National Park.

HEART REMEDY
JASMINE SMITH

DURING the hectic storm, society seemed to crumble and was beginning to collapse. The pastel grey in the sky was taken over by dark rain clouds, which turned the atmosphere entirely black. The trees swayed through the city as the wind changed patterns which became heavier and faster. It was the middle of winter, and Vancouver expected three deep feet of snow. The storm was monitored closely, as some residents were being evacuated from their houses and moved to Maryland High School for safety purposes. Emergency crews had been busy over the last week due to automotive accidents from the weather change. Lucas Taylor stared outside the window and held a newspaper and a coffee in each hand. The cover of the newspaper had a picture of the winter scenery. The article was telling people about the evacuation process. Lucas put the newspaper down, not paying attention to the details, and welcomed Allison to sit beside him. Allison and Lucas have been married for two years and both work at St. Evelyn hospital, located on the outskirts of North Vancouver. Allison had green eyes, and long auburn hair that she usually kept in a ponytail. She has been a doctor for four years, specializing in pediatric care at St. Evelyn. Lucas has worked as a cardiologist for six years, and has spoken to local universities about cardiology and how the heart works. Lucas had short, light brown hair and forest green eyes. Both Allison and Lucas were one of the many hundreds of families being forced to leave their houses when the storm picked up. The chaos of the storm had injured many, so the hospital's focus was on the newly admitted citizens. As a result, a small number of previous patients passed away from cardio-related illnesses. Out of interest and curiosity, Dr. Taylor had gone through the hospital records, only to find that the cardio-related cases doubled within the last 3 years. Allison took Lucas' left hand and asked, "Do you happen to know if there are any spots left for the CT scan?" In a displeasing voice he responded, "If there is one open you'd better book it now, because a nurse will take it. What's the rush?" Allison jumped to her feet and hurried out the door. "Well, one of the babies in pediatrics care has a little bit of a heart defect. I'm hoping to find out what was the cause and if it could become a problem in the future," her shaky voice echoed through the hallway. As Lucas said his good bye to Allison, he was interrupted.

"Okay sweetheart, I love y. . ."

"Doctor Taylor, we need you in the ER, stat! We have a man who has a case of severe heart failure, and you need to look at him immediately." A panicked nurse, helped pull a stretcher through the crowded hallway leading into the E.R. The male patient had a muscular build, with an oxygen mask over his mouth, which was being manually pumped by a nurse, while a paramedic was on top of him, giving him CPR.

"Okay, his heart rate's at sixty over twenty... he's going into cardiac arrest, someone get a crash cart!" Lucas was frantic as he yelled out directions to the nurses.

Later on that day, an unknown figure walked through the lounge door with the head doctor of St. Evelyn Hospital, Bill Roberts.

"Dr. Taylor, this is Dr. Mitchell Foley. He's one of our newly hired cardiologists. He has an impressive background, just as you do and that's part of the reason why I got him. You two will be great together. He has introduced us to a new procedure for patients specifically with heart problems," said Dr. Roberts. "Foley, you can go and check out the cafeteria. It's down this hallway to your left," said Dr. Roberts, who seemed to be in a jolly mood. Lucas responded, "Okay that sounds great. Just make sure he aids me in all the cases, to get an idea of what we do around here. Got that?"

"Of course," Bill replied sympathetically. Lucas walked away and left Bill standing there, with a smirk on his face

Lucas walked down the corridor, and took an elevator up to the fourth floor, where Allison was. He watched her through the glass window. He could never get enough of it. Whenever times got rough at work, Lucas would always walk upstairs to watch the doctors and nurses in pediatrics. Allison had always been good with kids, and to see her treat them with the friendliest smile and the gentlest touch, he knew was more than he could ever do.

Lucas looked up, and Allison signalled for him to meet her in the hallway. "I need you to do a surgery on Kaden," Allison said, pointing to a tiny baby boy, covered with wires and a feeding tube sticking out of his stomach. "He's the one I was talking about…you know the one with the defect?"

Lucas and Allison peered over Kaden. "Well, with the results being he has a small hole in his heart, the only option is to do surgery," Lucas replied. Allison had a worried expression on her face, and asked "What are the risks involved when he has the surgery?"

"The same as any other open heart surgery, Alli. The only difference is that we're dealing with an infant.

"Lucas…what do we do now?"

"We have to book the operating room and get a team of surgeons together… and by the way, has Roberts told you that he hired a new cardiologist?"

"No, have you met him yet?"

"Yes I have. I'll introduce you to him later. I have to talk to him first. You know, to make him feel welcomed, and get him to warm up a bit," Lucas responded.

"I'll talk to you later Alli, I love you."

"I love you too Lucas," said Allison.

Lucas went to the cafeteria to get a coffee and find Dr. Roberts, when he ran into the new cardiologist, Dr. Foley. "Hi, Foley isn't it?" Lucas asked with some hesitation in his voice. "Yes I am… you must be Lucas Taylor. I have learned so much about you. What is your… I mean our first case?" Lucas carefully stated "A baby boy, in the pediatrics wing, on the second floor. He is our main priority right now."

"Lucas, I was actually wondering when we can get into the operating room."

"I don't know I haven't needed to be in the O.R. lately, but I can tell you that we will need one for this patient."

"Okay, so I can perform my procedure on the baby," Foley asked, with concern.

"Well I haven't heard about it so we'll hold off on it. Is that okay?"

"Why would you waste time? We need to do it now! The procedure will work I promise."

"What is your so called procedure?" asked Lucas.

"We'll inject pre-programmed microbes, which are permitted to fix the patients heart and it works on any type of heart condition. We can do a scan, similar to a bone scan or CT scan, where we insert a special kind of dye into the patient, which will react with the microbes, to track them down to see how they are progressing. With the tests my company has run, it seems to work well. We have tried it on one patient that had a defect; there was a hole in her heart. After we injected the patient with the microbes, she had the heart of an athletic twenty year old," bragged Mitchell.

"Wow. That's an accomplishment."

"It feels good to try to help out these people. This way, they get better within a four day period."

"Impressive," Lucas said, with a stunned look on his face.

"Have you run this across Dr. Roberts?"

"Yes. He loved it," Dr. Foley replied.

"I'm not sure if we can start this quite yet. I have to go meet with someone so I'll catch up with you."

"Who are you meeting up with?"

"My wife," replied Lucas with a perfect smile across his face, and he began to blush. Lucas knew that every time he talked about Allison, he went red, and couldn't help but smile.

"You're wife works here?"

"Yes. You should come and meet her." Lucas and Mitchell began to walk to the elevator. As they were walking, Foley got a page from Dr. Roberts, suggesting that the two of them should meet up and discuss the new procedure. Foley and Taylor parted off to different directions.

Lucas ended up going from one floor to another looking for Allison. He found her as she was searching for him. She gazed at Lucas and asked, "Who's the new doctor?"

"Doctor Foley."

Lucas repeated exactly what Roberts had said to him. "We've been discussing this new procedure, which his company created. It sounds so crazy, but he and Roberts are going to try to get it approved by health services this week. I'm waiting to see what Bill thinks, because I personally haven't seen any reports, or have been convinced that this medical procedure actually works," Lucas said, with a worried look.

"Well… you don't know him too well, and I haven't even met him so let's not come to any conclusions and just see what happens. Got that? I really want to go home. It's been more than two days since we've been there. Ah…I miss sleeping in our own bed, and not having to suffer from the hard mattresses here. We should take some time off. We work so hard," Allison responded. A bit agitated, Lucas said "This is bothering me. I like the procedure, but I don't want to do anything illegal, or possibly hurt anyone."

"Get the permission forms, and use those. With the consent you can use this procedure and have a clear mind," reassured Allison. She and Lucas held hand in hand as they walked to the cafeteria. On the way, Lucas went to check out the doctors schedules. He was scheduled as an on call cardiologist, because his friend Steven was taking his place, when his regular shift ended. When the Taylor's entered the cafeteria, Lucas noticed Bill and Mitchell talking with each other. He could tell it was about something good, probably the procedure, after studying their faces. He grabbed on to

Allison's arm and started to walk their way over to the table. "Any word yet?" asked Lucas.

"Hello Lucas and Allison! I was just telling Mitchell that health services agreed to let us use the microbes. Before we start, Mitch will have to show you how it works," blurted out Dr. Roberts.

"That's great, but have you got any records, showing that the patient has reacted well to these microbes Mitchell?" asked Lucas.

"As a matter of fact, I believe I do." Dr. Foley quickly opened up his brief case, and pulled out the charts of a patient from a Toronto hospital. "This woman, suffered blockage throughout the arteries, and these microbes were specifically programmed for her needs. We produce plenty of micro-organisms, each a different purpose. For her case, the microbes without delay, started to attack the blockage. This way, if we use this procedure, it's more effective, and less of a risk of complications."

"Right now one of my patients is suffering from a hole in his heart, as well as an irregular heart beat," said Allison, looking fairly interested.

"Oh. I took a look at Kaden. He's the one, right?"

"Yes. Would this formula work on him?"

"Of course it would," replied Mitchell, as he stared into Allison's forest green eyes. Lucas saw the way Mitchell looked at his wife, but was cautious not to say anything. "When were you planning to start this system?" questioned Lucas.

"Well, I'll have to show you and you're lovely wife, how to insert these microbes. You have to make sure you grab the one with the proper label on it. There are different microbes for every heart problem. It's not that complicated and I'll be there for assistance of each patient you use them on," stated Dr. Foley. In an over ruling way, Dr. Roberts said, "I believe we should start these procedures as soon as we can. How does tomorrow work for everyone?" Dr. Roberts went through a circular pattern asking each doctor if it was okay, and everyone agreed.

It was the following day, and another restless night for the Taylor's. Sleeping on a flat and hard bunk, in the on call room was affecting their sleep patterns quite a bit. They woke up at around five A.M. and the snow was still coming down hard. As they left the room, Lucas received a page from Mitchell, informing him of a one-on-one meeting in the cafeteria. Lucas had thoughts running through his head all night long. He thought about the way Mitch's eyes gazed upon Alli, and the tone he used when he spoke to her, but he dismissed the thoughts, telling himself that Mitchell was just being kind, just as Alli was always a polite and very nice person. Lucas decided not to accuse him of anything. At the cafeteria, Mitch had lined up three coffees on the table. While drinking one of his own, he said "Why didn't you bring Allison?"

"She had to go up to the pediatric care unit. I can see if she wants to join us," Lucas replied.

"Well, I'm going to be educating you two and a couple others about the procedure and the tools involved, in about twenty minutes. Drink your coffee, bring Allison and meet me in the cardiology department," stated an over joyful Mitchell. Lucas ran up to Allison's floor and delivered the coffee to her. He told her about the training plan and she agreed to be there. Lucas promised to meet her on the first floor, near the gift shop before the training started.

Once the Taylor's met up at the gift shop, they both headed up to the cardiology department. As they arrived, Bill Roberts, Mitchell Foley, and Steven Kelley, were all waiting. They got down to business, as Mitch explained how to complete the procedures. The first patient on the list received the microbes that would start unblocking her arteries. Dr. Foley started by introducing himself, as well as the other doctors. "You start out by filling the syringe with the serum containing the microbes, and finding a healthy vein to inject it into. You then keep the patient under observation, just as a caution. If they are fine, you give them a scan then release them. I take it everyone understands? If you are going to give these serums to patients, you need to let me know first," advised Foley. The doctors started to leave the room when Mitchell pulled Allison and Lucas aside. "Lucas you have a patient waiting in the room next to us that needs the repairing microbes, and Alli, you have Kaden to help. I'll give you both the product to use," Mitchell said impatiently. Lucas walked through the door, and walked into the next room to deal with a new patient. Lucas filled the syringe, and poked the needle into the man's vein. He explained to him how the procedure would work. "This is advanced medicine, really incredible. It's the type of procedure that will save thousands of people each year, including yourself," Lucas blurted out confidently. As Lucas co-operated with his patient, Allison was having some troubles between herself and Kaden's parents. "If you would just listen to me for one minute, then I can explain everything."

"We have been. If you would just listen to us," snapped back the mother.

"Okay. I am listening."

"Our religious views strongly believe that it is not right for our child to get treated with this medicine. It is against our wishes, as well as our lords that Kaden receives this treatment. And that's the final decision," said the father. Allison had the needle in her right hand and when she reached for the child, the mother quickly grabbed Allison. The grapple caused the needle to inject into Allison's side. She was in complete shock and didn't know exactly what to do. The nurses assisting looked at her confused and concerned. One of the nurses, Chaylene, who was a close friend of Allison's, helped her sit down on an empty bed. It was twenty five minutes later until every one had finally calmed down from the scene. Chaylene continued to comfort Alli and discuss the procedure, but immediately noticed that her pupils became dilated, and she began to slur her words. Chaylene paged Lucas in a panic, as a cherry-red coloured rash had spread   all over Allison's skin.

The moment Lucas received the page, he ran to see what was happening with Allison right away. Lucas saw Chaylene and other doctors and nurses huddled over, working on Allison who stopped breathing. Her heart rate began dropping by the second. "Chay, what happened?" asked Lucas who took out a stethoscope and placed it on Alli's chest trying to get a heartbeat.

"She was stabbed with the syringe filled with the new microbe procedure serum. She just lost consciousness, she's going into cardiac arrest, get the paddles!"

"Come on Alli, wake up, you'll be fine," Lucas said, as he started to choke up. Tears rolled down his face as he felt helpless watching his wife fight for her life. "So this is what it's like for a patient's family," he whispered to himself. Lucas didn't want to leave Alli's side no matter what, but he quickly realized the one person who would know what to do would be Mitchell. He kissed Allison on her forehead and left the room, while the doctors got her heart beating again. Lucas rushed down the hallways screaming "Foley!" He was upset in all the ways he could possibly be. He was mad at Foley, Roberts, himself, Alli, and the hospital. Lucas spotted Mitchell from the corner of his eye, and sped up his pace over towards him. "You're microbes are killing my wife. It's not safe! Do you understand? It's killing my wife! You need stop all of the procedures."

"Calm down Lucas, what's going on?" said Bill, as he walked out of his office. "The genius plan- Your genius plan… is killing Allison. She nearly died. She might die," With his eyes watering, and his throat closing he managed to get those words out.

"Why did she take it?" asked Mitchell.

"She… she didn't, she was in a bit of an argument, and the boy's mother fell into her. Alli received the end of the needle into her side."

Panicking, Mitchell said, "Okay. We need to inject her with a dye, and get her straight to a CT scan. There's no waiting."

Worried, Lucas asked, "Okay, what will that do?"

"It will show us where the microbes are and what they are doing to her heart. Right now Lucas, I think you should be by your wife's side."

"I can't… I have to help her."

"But you would be helping her. You would let her know you are there for her, let her know that you're supporting her. Okay?" Dr. Roberts said trying to console him.

"Why don't you guys understand? We should have done more tests and research before releasing this treatment to the public."

"Lucas, I'm sorry. Just go be at Allison's side," Bill said apologetically. Lucas sat there in the room, while Mitchell and the other doctors took Allison down to get the CT scan. As they were gone, Lucas sat on the chair and fidgeted with his hands. Fifteen minutes later, the results had come back, and they found the microbes were attacking her heart even though she was perfectly healthy before. "We have to stop these pests from eating away the rest of her heart," stated Dr. Foley. "Well how do we do that?" asked Bill. Chaylene had walked back from the imagery room, and sat down next to Mitchell. "Right now, she's stable, but we don't think for much longer. Is there any medication we can give her? How do we get rid of the microbes?"

Mitchell replied, "Well, we might have a serum we made that might eat away at the microbes. What is supposed to happen with the serum is to release the microbes to fix the heart. What seemed to have happened was since her heart was already fine, they ate away at the healthy heart to fix it after it had done the damage. We may have some of the antidote at the office in Abbotsford. I'll make a call. In the meantime, stick her on all of the heart monitors. Keep track of her medications. I'm so sorry Lucas; I'll make this up to both of you. I promise," Mitchell said in an upset tone of voice. With no hesitation, Dr. Foley lifted the receiver of the telephone, and began to talk to a doctor within his company. Foley ordered him to send the antidote, and once all the heart patients he's helped are retreated with the antidote, he's shutting down the business because it's too risky and every time the microbes do their jobs, they tear the heart up, then heal it again. The more times the microbes do this, the riskier the procedures become and death is close. Mitchell ran out of the office yelling 'They've got a helicopter, coming here to drop of the remedy. Once Allison gets the antidote into her system, her heart should start to go back to normal after half an hour." Lucas got up and rushed out the doors, and went straight for the roof top, where the helicopter landing pad was. His heart was beating so fast that he thought it might blow a fuse.

It took at least fifteen minutes for the helicopter to get to the hospital and land. The serum only took ten minutes to get Allison to breathe on her own, and kept her heart rate steady. Her rash began to disappear, and she started to act a bit like herself again. "What happened?"

"Do you remember the argument?" asked Lucas.

"Yes…with Kaden's parents."

"You were accidently injected with the microbe serum. Because you had a healthy heart, the microbes did as they were programmed, except for the fact that you had a healthy heart so it attacked the heart just to fix it, then it just repeated the cycle," Lucas stated quickly.

Dr. Roberts had stopped by Allison's room to see how Lucas and she were coping. "How is she?" Roberts asked, in a concerned manner.

"She's recovering to a large extent. We gave her an antidote that Mitchell kept at his office incase something like this would happen, and it helped out a lot."

"Well that's good. I can't have my top doctors sick, get better soon Allison," said Roberts.

"Thanks," whispered Allison, exhaustedly.

Dr. Foley constantly apologized to both Allison and Lucas. Lucas pulled Mitchell out of the room and into the hall. He wasn't upset about his role as part of the chaos. He was bothered that the reason why it attacked her heart so rapidly was because it was a perfect, healthy heart. "I'm sorry, for insulting you and your treatment, but for the record, you're idea was the smartest thing I've heard of, even though it doesn't work for everything," laughed Lucas. Dr. Foley became Allison's doctor during her recovery stay at the hospital. One patient had unfortunately passed away from a bad reaction to the microbes. Once Allison heard about it, she became a bit traumatized, but she was thankful she was still alive. She was released from the hospital a week later, and the Taylor's received three weeks off of work.

During the last of the winter month, the snow disappeared and the rain poured down. The sun shined once again, and life ceased to be hectic.

IN THE LINE OF DUTY
AARON COLE

IN panic, Robert tore his mask off in complete horror, fully knowing that he would be breathing nothing but treacherous smoke. He pulled frantically at his mask, hoping to regain that last breath while he anxiously searched for a way out of the smoke filled room.

...

Kayla was in the kitchen late at night, when she heard a knock on the door. She quickly rushed over in hopes it would be her husband coming home after the call he had received a few hours earlier. She was very supportive of her husband's career, but she would always worry about him when he got called out. She could never sleep knowing he was in danger, so if he ever got called out, she was most likely checking out the repeat episodes of *The Late Show*, or watching a late night flick. She loved to play with her long black hair, while she was up at night. Her heart dropped when she saw the two men standing on the porch. She opened the door to get a better look. She noticed that both of them were wearing their station uniforms, something that you rarely saw outside of the hall, and that they were holding their hats over their hearts. She had been to many events with the firefighters and knew most of them, and these two she recognized as part of Robert's team. The tall man on the right, wearing a name tag that read "McDonald", spoke first. "Ma'am, I regret to inform you that your husband has been killed in the line of duty. Robert had gone into the fire using the new F-series cylinders; we have related that your husband's death was caused by the new advanced series. The advanced SCBA tank took the wrong reading on your husband and would no longer release air." He seemed to have a piercing tone, as every word hurt Kayla more and more. The man went on about how her husband was a brave man, but Kayla's mind was in pieces. She had known that her husband's career was hazardous, but she refused to believe something like this could happen. A thousand thoughts filled her at once. She had told her husband she didn't like that he was relying on advanced equipment for his life and that good old fashioned stuff worked just as good. She never did like knowing of the dangers involved in the new packs. Kayla never did like new technology, but Robert welcomed it. All she could think in her head was that if she had made him listen he would be here at the door and not these men. "Ma'am?" the man on the left asked. Kayla quickly realized she had disappeared in her own thoughts. As she tried to hold back her tears she thanked the men and told them she would be in touch. Trying to hold back her tears was harder than swallowing broken glass. She thanked them and closed the door as the two walked back to the truck. She immediately ran upstairs, no longer able to hold in her tears, and opened the door to their baby's bedroom. She picked up her little boy, whose eyes had the same sparkle that Robert's had. Holding Robert close, she knew in her heart she could never let anything bad happen to her son.

"I always have to yell at him to get up. He is always late for school unless I kick him out of bed. He always forgets his alarm clock. He's forgetful like his dad. He is an enthusiastic kid and he is very energetic, but he hates mornings. Robbie is so much like his father." She told her therapist while lying on her couch. The therapist had to come to Kayla's house because in Dr. Baron's building there was a new type of elevator Kayla wouldn't use. Kayla had been seeing Dr. Baron for four years, but he could never get her to talk about her problem. She always shrugged it off and continued to talk about Robert Jr.

Robbie was one year old when the accident took place. She saw Dr. Baron twice a week for the first year and once a week after that. It was three years before Kayla told Robert what happened to his dad. Whenever Robbie would ask, "Why does Billy have a daddy and a mommy but I only have a mommy?" Kayla would tell him he did, he was just in another place, and immediately changed the subject. Every night after

Kayla told Robbie about his dad, she would tell him a new story before she tucked him in at night.

Robbie was very mature for five years old. Dr. Baron talked to Robbie one day and explained to him what his mom was going through, so when she told him the same story twice before bedtime, he acted just as excited as the first time. Robbie didn't like that his mom wouldn't have anything to do with high-tech equipment. All his friends had the latest game systems and toys, but he wasn't allowed to have anything more than a TV with a VCR and some old Disney movies. Kayla saw more and more of her husband in Robert every day, especially when Robert made his mom pull the car over because he saw someone trip and he wanted to make sure they were okay. She loved that about her husband: he always wanted to help, no matter what the cost. When Kayla saw things like this in her son, it secretly scared her. She feared that one day he would become like his dad, putting his life in danger to help other people. She was terrified that she would lose him as well.

Kayla liked to go for runs, and Robbie would often join her. They usually ran around the park nearby. Robbie would regularly ask his mom to take him to the fire hall, but she never would for two reasons: after the funeral for her husband, she had cut off contact with the fire hall completely for fear of reminder. She was also afraid her son might like what he saw, and one day becomes a firefighter as well. That scared her more than anything.

One afternoon they were doing the usual laps around the park when Kayla noticed the shortness of breath in her son. She brushed it off as if it were nothing. A couple of weeks later she started to notice it more and more, so she decided to stop taking him with her for a while. She felt bad that he had to stay at home while she was out so she decided to pick him up another Disney movie or two at the old run-down movie shop a few blocks past the park. She picked up a few movies that she knew he would like. She rushed home as it was starting to get cold out and she was eager to give Robbie his surprise. On her way home, she was observing how she couldn't walk down the street without noticing some sort of new piece of machinery that didn't exist seven years ago. She got in the front door and called for him, but he did not come. She figured he was in his room watching a movie or sleeping so she tiptoed upstairs as not to disturb him. When she got upstairs, all she saw was her son on the floor drenched in blood.

It seemed like forever. Robert Keller Jr. and his mom sat in the room, waiting for the test results. Kayla had been so worried about her son that she didn't even notice she had been in a car that was driven by a computer, and at the hospital she was lifted to her son's room in an air lifted elevator. It was just another advancement since Robert's death. They had to stay in the room for three weeks and Robert Jr. was worried he would miss Christmas, which was only two weeks away. The hospital wouldn't let Robbie go because they wanted to keep him under close observation. His mom, of course, would not leave his side. Losing her patience one morning, Kayla got up and was about to storm out to find some answers when their family doctor walked in with her son's chart. She calmly sat back down in the chair that was set beside her son's bed. The doctor asked if he could talk to Kayla in private. She walked out of the room, letting the doctor lead the way.

"I'm going to be honest with you Mrs. Keller; we've done the tests and double checked them to make sure they were analyzed properly. Your son has a cancerous tumor growing in his lung. This is a very rare case for such a young child, but we have decided that his body has not developed enough for the radiation therapy. The only way to help him is to remove the tumor from his lung. Doing this, though, has many complications with such a young child. Chances are that a successful procedure can only promise him, under good circumstances, two years to live. After the procedure there is nothing we can do for him but ease his pain. The procedure is very safe, as it is run now by robotic arms that have been programmed perfectly. If the procedure goes a hundred percent there is one thing we may be able to do for Robert Jr. There has been a lot of research put into telomerase and we have come up with a treatment for the replacing of the cells that the cancer kills. But again, Mrs. Keller, there is a complication with using this on such a young child. If we give your son the enzyme it will have a 50/50 shot of working. If it doesn't work, there is a greater chance that it will kill him within a few months. If the shot works, then your son's DNA will grow back where the cancer has been removed and he will be a healthy kid again. It's a very technological advancement that we're proud of, but it has never been used on anyone under the age of thirty." Kayla had the same look on her face she did when she was given the news about her husband. Only this time the thoughts going through her head were involving the risk of what little time he might have. Saying nothing, she walked back to the room where her baby boy was sitting anxiously to find out what his mom knew. She sat beside him with the same feeling of swallowing glass as she tried to keep from breaking into tears. She told her son what was wrong with him. She told him the only cure was never tested on someone as young as him and he may only have as much as two years left. She told him that the surgery was done by a computer based system with robotic arms. He kind of giggled at the thought of that, and when Kayla looked into her son's eyes, she saw that sparkle; the same one that her husband had in his eyes when he said "I love you" to her. She saw the man reaching out to her and asking her to forgive. Robbie grabbed her hand and asked if, when it was all over, she could take him to the fire hall. Just like his dad, he always wanted to go to the hall.

"Merry Christmas little fella," bellowed a tall man with a

name tag that read "McDonald." "Where you been the last 4 years? We have needed a junior firefighter on the team. Would you like to become an honorary member?" asked McDonald at the Christmas Eve party at the old fire hall. Though the hall was not very big, they managed to fit everybody in to the crowded room. Excitedly, he looked at his mom for approval, who was being handed something by the other firefighter she recognized from that dreadful night. When she walked over to him, he noticed she was holding a helmet that read "Keller" on the back. His mom bent down to give her boy a kiss, then placed the helmet on his head and told him she'd love it if he joined.

KARMA IS A BITCH
PJ OLUND

DON'T worry,
about a thing.
'Cause every little thing,
is gonna be alright
-"Three Little Birds" Bob Marley

"Change the song." I said, annoyed by the sound of Kimya Dawson's "cute singing" blasting out of our only I-Pod.

"No!" Selena said. "You've had the I-Pod every time we're out on patrol. I think it's only fair that I'd get a shot."

"Not every time." I said with a hint of denial.

"Yes, I'm pretty sure you have," she said. "And every time you do, it's always the same dumbass playlist that's made up of Metallica, Joy Division and Nine Inch Nails."

"Those aren't the only bands that are on there." I said, trying to defend my comrades of rock from utter extinction, in the hands of the music that "cool" teenage girls listen to.

"What else?" Selena asked. "Bob Marley and 'I Touch Myself'?"

"Only Bob Marley." I admit I put on 'Three Little Birds' for the sake of trying to help us keep our sanity. "Our" meaning Selena, Dante, Mike, and myself. Mike and Dante are back at the stronghold.

"Sure," she said sarcastically. "Face it; you're Über repressed because that chick you were with was one of the possible billion that died from the malfunction."

"No, I am not!" I boomed, even though she's right. "Besides, Teresa was flashing her shit all over town behind my back. I could care less if she got her limbs ripped off and eaten right in front of me. She probably enjoyed it."

"That's great, Rob." Selena said, disgusted. "Really necessary."

"At least I'm not afraid to talk about it." I said, making reference to her former partner.

Selena was baffled by my statement. "What's that supposed

to mean?" she asked, in a fuming manner.

"C'mon," I said, wanting to give her some of her own medicine. "How did what's her face, that you were sleeping with die?" Selena doesn't like it when someone makes a reference to her deceased love, so I knew it would make her fall into a similar position to my own.

"Don't be a dick." she said in a very frail tone of voice. "You know I don't like to talk about it."

"Well, now you know how I feel." I said. I have her now.

"Ok fine," she said, feeling really guilty. "Sorry for being a bitch."

"You're forgiven," I said. After a bit of a pause I said, "Seriously though, what was her name?"

"Up yours, buddy."

Conversations like this are ever present being around people like Selena for so long. Especially while walking around a deserted, and apocalyptic wasteland version of Seattle, with a Colt CAR-15 slung on your back going to get some food.

I guess that's the cue for me to explain why Seattle, home of Grunge, Starbucks and the highest junkie population in the United States, is in this state of mass destruction and utter extinction. Well, see this is a very complicated matter and I'm not very good with telling stories, but I'll try my best 'cause I like you so much.

It all started about three years ago when this guy, Weston Scott; a British businessman, decided that he and his company (Scott Corporation) should invest in the growing industry of nano technology. You know, when you put computers inside of yourself to give the body a "little break". If the body and its organs/cells are the blue collar workers, nano technology are the Mexicans.

Anyway, his company began to develop this computer, which could be implanted into your brain, and could allow you to download and upload information into your brain.

Needless to say, a good portion of the world decided to spend the $777,000 that it went for at Best Buy. Of course, struggling 20 something's like myself, couldn't afford it. Wasted too much on bongs and rare Black Flag singles.

Ok, I'm going to stop doing that. I have a habit of trailing off when I tell stories.

Within a matter of months, Scott was making more money than Trump and Bill Gates combined. He even got *Time*'s Entrepreneur of the Year award. He was so popular that politicians like Obama and Kim Jong-Il were asking him personally to build one to their specifications. There was one problem however. Last December, a sudden vi-

"Hold up," Selena said.

Bitch cut me off in the middle of an important plot device.

"Animal. Up ahead." We ducked down and hid behind a car. 'Animal' is our name for the poor, mindless shmucks that infest most of the city. They prey on whatever form of flesh they can get their hands on. Their very rare to see, but very deadly. And one of them was right in front of the Safeway.

He was once a middle aged gentleman, with a possible wife and honour roll kids, at Fincher Elementary School. Now he was nothing but a cruel reminder of the baby steps of mankind. He growled and huffed as he searched for food of some kind, something to satisfy his hunger. He rummaged through the garbage outside the entrance, sniffing at anything that caught his eye, or looked somewhat edible. Clearly, the creature was really hungry.

"What should we do?" I whispered. Selena tried to think of something reasonable and smart, something to keep us both from losing any limbs. "Kill it, maybe." She replied.

"Scratch that," I said, "Others might hear the shot. I say we wait."

"No," Selena said, "It's gonna get dark soon. We gotta get

rid of him."

"Don't be stupid!" I slightly yelled. The creature turned his head around, making a low growl and staring out with his albino eyes. Both me and Selena stopped moving and were dead quiet, but he knew we were there. It was only a matter of seconds before he would lunge out and make our worlds turn red.

A noise went off to the west of us. The creature noticed it, quickly turning his head. Before long, the creature sped off from sight to investigate the disturbance. Selena and I waited for a moment and then breathed a sigh of relief. Thank god, we thought. Though from what has happened in the last 8 months, I'm starting to question his presence.

I used the key I obtained working as a rent a cop at the store before the malfunction. I was struggling to find the right key. "Every time, man." I said. I finally got the right one and we made our way inside. The lights are on as usual. Selena grabbed a cart and we began the usual trek around the store.

It has always been the same list whenever we go:
- 3 jugs of 2% Milk
- Cheddar Cheese
- Variety pack of Mac N' Cheese
- Starbucks House Blend
- Soap
- Selsum Blue shampoo
- 6 Pack of Rainier Beer
- Energizers
- Hustler (for the guys)
- Curve (for Selena)

While wandering around the store, I noticed a copy of the Jeff Buckley album *Grace* in the discount rack, something I had never noticed before. "Think I'll take this." I told Selena.

"Don't you already have that CD?" She asked.

"No," I said, "Don't think so."

"Who is that guy anyway? Everybody seems to like him."

I felt like going Jack Black on her, but I decided to play it cool. "Oh, he was amazing. He only put out one album and then died in a swimming accident."

"Tragic."

"Oh yeah. He's a hell of a singer, though. If Jesus could sing, he'd sound like him."

Selena laughed at the comment. "He's that good, huh?"

"Yeah," I said, "We'll listen to it when we get back."

We finished up and made our way out of the store, passing that all too familiar newspaper rack, with that all too familiar headline:

TERROR IN SEATTLE:

THE HORROR! THE HORROR!

PROJECT REASON
CHRISTIAN PHILLIPS

I anxiously picked up an old, broken pencil. The lead was dull and the paper I had was stained. My hand shook as the footsteps echoed in my ears. I began to write a desperate plea: If anyone can read this I am already dead. They come for us. Don't let them take it. Tell Cindy; no. The evidence is in the chest.

I work at the Scientific Developments Lab in New York on a government project. The project is focused on examining why people believe in religion and how to make them understand that science is the only true way of reasoning for anything. It is called Project Reason. Right now I was in charge of examining the difference in neurological activities between theists and atheists. It was important that people know the futility of believing in a fictional deity. There is neither time nor place for a man's frustrated attempts at finding God. The scientific advances we have made are from those willing to ignore the wasted efforts of lost minds, and encourage the men who feed their brain the nutrients of knowledge.

It was time for me to head home. Graveyard shifts seem timeless in the labs. 12 hours of tedious research. I retrieved my coat from my locker. Above the staff lockers was a large white sign that read, 'The World our Body'. I lived by those words. They reminded all of us that what we are doing is necessary, like a body that removes unwanted material from itself. We are the necessary balance that this world requires. I opened the lab door and walked down the hall towards the exit; it wasn't too busy in the early morning. Luckily, I got to avoid some of my annoying co-workers. A lot of people I worked with, like Joel in my department, are more fanatical about science than some of the religious activists I've seen on TV. My car was in pretty rough shape, but it got me places. Ever since the government put in Project Reason there have been so many scientists that the demand was very low, so I didn't make too much money.

On my way home I decided to stop for a drink. After a bumpy ride, due to my useless shocks, I arrived at Jamie's Tavern. I cursed and slowly found a place to park. I was opening my door and grabbing my keys, when an old man rushed out of the tavern with his arms flailing in the air. He started yelling, "Help! Help me, oh please sir!" I rushed to his assistance. "Hey! What do you need, what's wrong?"

"My son, he is hurt, please you must help me. I cannot help him I am too weak." He panicked.

"Where is he?"

"The basement! Please, come!"

I was very tired, but something compelled me to help him. He motioned me to follow him inside the tavern. We rushed towards the basement door. He or his son was obviously the owner of the place as there was no one at the till. As we crept downstairs I saw a large man in a suit beating a younger man. It was hard for me to make out any details, as the lights were dim. I didn't know what to do, but the old man was urging me on. I saw a crowbar on the ground and picked it up. Not sure of myself, I swung it at the man in the suit. I missed and he grabbed my neck and delivered a swift knee to my ribcage. I looked up as a giant fist was thrown towards my face. I leaned to the left and offered a solid hit to the man's face with the crowbar. The massive agent was instantly knocked out. I dropped the crowbar and the old barkeep and I attended the younger man. We heard more guys coming, figuring that they were more suited guys, and hurried. "Thank you so much for saving me sir." He coughed some blood, and then looked at me, "Please meet me and my father at Cindy's Salon later today on 6th and Main." Before I could reply they fled through the door on the left. I soon followed as I wasn't about to run into any more of those guys. Before I left, however, I looked at the man I had knocked out. On his vest were tiny letters stitched in silver, 'The World our Body'.

I got in my car and drove home quickly; the men had

obviously entered the building when I had left, for I couldn't see them outside. I was so confused about the whole incident that happened; why was that man working for us and beating that younger guy? Why was there more coming? I had hoped it was some sort of rogue agent group. I figured I should ask the Lead Development Manager, George Howell. He knew a lot and he was able to help me before with less serious questions. I also trusted him as a friend. When I got into my apartment, I picked up the phone and called him. "Hey George, you got any time?"

"Is this Alex? Oh what a pleasure you called, you know I was just about to go out, good thing you caught me! What did you need?"

"I just had some questions about the project. I know a lot about what's going on in my lab but not much else. What is going on in the outside world in terms of Project Reason?" The tone in his voice changed drastically, it was almost unrecognizable, "Only what is needed to be done Alex."

"Are we hurting anybody, George?"

"We are simply... fixing them. They are brainwashed Alex, brainwashed idiots."

"Are we hurting them!?"

"The world is our body and like a body we must make... sacrifices." I then hung up on him. What on earth was that all about? He usually is very good at explaining things, but he was obviously hiding something from me.

I found myself driving up to Cindy's salon. It was a nice place; the wooden exterior gave it a homely feel. A beautiful girl at the front counter looked at me, "Hello darlin', you here for a snip?" She had a raw Texan accent. "No, I just—", she moved her hand under the counter and a door to the left opened up. She smiled and motioned for me to go there. I walked down some stairs to a dusty basement where about ten or so people were sitting on crates and chairs and a man with a symbol of a shield on his jacket stood. He was clearly talking to them before I had come in, but he stopped before I could know what he was talking about. His wrinkly face sunk a bit as he looked at me and smiled, "Ah, the protector! I heard you were coming. Saved Rupert didn't you?"

"Uh, yes he was being hurt. I'm sorry what is—"

"As is common in this oppressing time."

"What do you mean?"

"What do I mean? Look around you young man, it is just as the dry days. The might of him will wash over us again" He looked down, "But until then we must suffer."

"You're not making any sense, and my name is Alex Glen."

"Sorry, Mr. Glen. The beast is making its move. The second-coming is impending. Now we just wait and pray—I mean talk, we wait and talk." He was obviously trying to cover up something, he was using odd metaphors and either he was mentally unstable or he was running something here. I was confused, very confused, "Who... who are you people and who does that man help?"

"Do you have faith in the government?" Came a familiar voice, it was Cindy. She was standing on the stairs. I looked at her. "Put your trust not in the government, as it only moves its people to condemnation." Preached the man with the shield symbol, I averted my attention to him. "Wait a second... are you guys some sort of religious organization?"

"Organization? Foolish man. We are the saved ones, and we follow only the 'organization' of the book and our Lord and Saviour."

"Project Reason has destroyed all bibles and they are destroying all your churches."

He looked at me heavily, "They will kill us as well." He then looked towards his people with a swelled chest, "The arms of men can only destroy our flesh, not our spirit. The copies of the bible are gone, yes, but the law does not permit the destruction of the bible in the museums. We will find one, and we will make copies for us all as long as the Lord is willing."

"I'm out of here; you all are living dangerous lives for no reason." As I turned to leave, the pastor said something to me that stuck, "Your false rhetoric will not shift the judgement of God, as it has the feeble minds of men. May the light be with you Alex." I turned my head towards the exit, walked up the stairs passed Cindy and left the salon.

I walked back to my car and to my dismay I realised that I had left the keys inside. I locked myself out. I cursed angrily and then decided to just walk home and call a tow truck. On my way back to my apartment; I saw a bunch of frightened people running around a corner crying, all with the same shield symbol as the pastor on their shirts. Then two suited men followed them, each armed with magnums. Then, one of the *suits* shot at them, piercing a shield-bearer's head. He dropped on the ground and that moment was carved in my mind. Immediately, I sprinted back to my condo.

I turned on my computer and opened up internet explorer. I searched about religion and God, but no results came up. Project Reason had erased everything. Even illegal sites were somehow stripped of their information. I was then compelled to start a journal. I wrote the events that had happened that day. I wrote how George talked to me on the phone, how the pastor was so sure of himself, how the young man was shot as well and about the other religious men who were pursued. I marked the date, July 4th, 2019. I got undressed out of my work clothes and went to my bed. Images of all that happened to the faithful people flashed in my head, and I began to cry. I needed to go back to that salon; I needed to talk to that pastor. I will go first thing tomorrow morning, I thought, before sleep overwhelmed me.

The next morning I went back to the salon, making sure to clutch my keys hard as I got out of my car. Entering the door I realised Cindy wasn't there. In fact, the room was destroyed, all the nice decorations that were on the walls and counters had been thrown off and shattered. I walked towards the counter seeing a few envelopes on the desk. Oddly enough, there was one with my name on it. I opened it and it read, 'Alex, I know I don't know you very well and neither did the people of this church. There was something about you that made you seem like an intelligent man, and the pastor agreed. I know you are confused. If you ever see me again, I wanted to know if you still believed in the government.' To tell you the truth, I wasn't sure. After all this happening I really was confused about who or what I worked for. I headed for the basement door.

Downstairs a wave of emotion hit me; every one of the church people was killed. They all lay dead on the floor. "No!" I screamed. Tears flooded my eyes as I ran towards the pastor's corpse. How could Project Reason do this? What was happening? I looked upon his corpse. He had a book that was titled, 'Evidence'. There were many pages but all were blank except for the first ten or so. They were journals of the people who had been going to the gathering here. It was all about their testimonies about their lives with God, and how he had helped them through their hard times. It had messages that God had shared with them and other things that made me reminiscent to when I was a child and I read a bit of a bible that was in a hotel. I tore through them desperately and stumbled upon one in particular. One entry read, 'My good friend Roberta Glen was murdered today. May the Lord watch over her, she was so faithful. The one final test came as a heartbreaking experience to us, but we must remember that it was her salvation and time of redemption. God bless.' My eyes widened as I read it over and over. Once again I started crying profusely. That was my wife! Instantly, I realised that when I was told that she had been hit by a car, it was a lie-- Project Reason killed her! They made that false death. They lied to their own person. Project Reason murdered Roberta! We murdered Roberta... I murdered Roberta. I fell on my knees and cried so hard, yelling out curses and screams. Then, like a warm blanket, I felt a hand on my shoulder. No one was there. Instantly I had an undoubting belief in God.

Once I recovered from the emotional trauma I drove to the Research and Development lab. I walked inside. Surprisingly it wasn't fury that I felt, but pity for those in here still trying to abolish people's beliefs. I went into George's office. I walked up to his desk and he smiled. "Alex, it's great to see you. Are you still confused about that whole outside work thing, because I know how to answer you now."

"No, George, I came here to put in my resignation."

"Wait a second, wait a second. Alex, you aren't serious are you?"

"I cannot work for Project Reason anymore. I am sorry."

"What? You can't just walk in and out of here like it's some sort of country club!" He yelled, and then stood up over me, "You sit down right now!" I had never seen George like this before; he had always been such a friendly person. "No, I am leaving this place and that's final!"

"So what? You think you found Jesus now? You idiot, there is no such thing as God. I am your God, Alex; the Government is your God. You will come in tomorrow morning and work your regularly scheduled shift or believe you me; you will be the same to us as the rest of those mindless morons!" He was sweating profusely and there was anger in his eyes unlike anything I had ever witnessed. His body was bent over the desk and his fists were clenched.

"Goodbye George." I walked out of his office; even after the door was closed I could hear him yell.

Over the next several months I had been evading the government, trying to make as little excitement as possible. I began to write journals. I was motivated by an out of this world force. They were all about my testimonies, what God had been saying to me and stories about the people I had helped. I had learned so much about the government by talking to people, old friends from work and new friends. While any religion had been a secret, anyone who was religious knew the others. It was so surprising to see how many people stood for their belief amidst the terror that was going on around them. People donated a lot of money when I told them I was writing about the works of God. It helped me live while I wasn't working. We had a secret lingo between us; now I understood what the pastor was talking about back then. He referred to the government as the beast, as it did in the bible during revelations. The second-coming was when Christ was going to come back and offer salvation to the faithful and judgement to the ungodly. No longer do our people dwell in freedom, we are forced to kneel and submit. It was like the old days when people had to use the sign of the fish to tell the Christians from the non Christians. Just like them, we used the shield to signify the protection God gave us. After I had completed the book I could only think of one name; Reasons. The name was in spite of the project and it told people that they could find some reasoning to believe by reading the book. For evidence, as I found out, wasn't just in the bible. It wasn't always in another's testimonies. It was a lot of times in your experiences with God. Although the government was trying to thwart our efforts; we, the hidden church, were making progress.

After I collected all my journals I published them into one book. I sent it out freely to people around the world. It was heard globally, and soon enough people started sharing their journals and books. Their books were like mine, full of their testimonies and God-motivated teachings. I got hundreds of them. After finding the best ones I decided to make a book out of them, a bible. Unfortunately, by then the government caught onto what I was doing. George obviously told them about why I resigned.

While I was putting the last books together, I heard a large vehicle outside my condo. I looked outside, several suited men came out. They all came for the lower floor. The elevator was busted so it bought me time. I couldn't get this book out to everyone, so I had to find another way of telling people about the evidence of God. I phoned my friend Elaine. She was not a believer, but told me she would do anything for me after the tragic death of my wife. She wasn't home so I left a message, 'Elaine, please, I don't have much time. In 3 days come to my house and open the third drawer down in my desk. There will be a note. Tell everyone you know about it, and understand it for yourself too, but be careful, and don't let the Government know about it—I don't have time to explain. Goodbye Elaine.' I wanted to tell people they could find evidence of God in their experiences, in their hearts, but the soldiers of Project Reason that had come to get me wouldn't understand it and destroy the note. Elaine was a smart girl; I knew she would be able to figure it out eventually. I wanted to meet that beautiful girl from the salon again, she reminded me of my wife. In all fairness I thought I should let her know that I was a believer in God now, not the government. She wanted to know. I wanted everyone to know that the government is corrupt and evil and not let them take their faith. I heard the footsteps coming near my door. I anxiously picked up an old, broken pencil. The lead was dull and the paper I had was stained. My hand shook as the footsteps echoed in my ears. I began to write a desperate plea: If anyone can read this I am already dead. They come for us. Don't let them take it. Tell Cindy; no. The evidence is in the chest.

RUNAWAY DNA
APRIL JOHNSON

THE date was current. Throughout the ages, harvested seeds were saved every season by farmers and growers alike. Since they were considered forms of life not open for patent registration, because of all the different variations, a threat arose when Genetically Modified (GM) seeds were developed. This allowed biotechnology to be patented, producing herbicide resistant seeds. It took scientists decades to realize that DDT, or Dichloro-Diphenyl-Trichloroethane, one of the best known synthetic chemical pesticides with a long and controversial history, might have hormonal changes that affected humans; in particular, the female hormone that controlled the reproductive cycle. It was used effectively among global populations, including the military during World War II, to control mosquitoes spreading malaria and lice transmitting typhus, resulting in dramatic reductions in both diseases. Cancer causing properties in DDT, created havoc with our health, which also reached our wildlife, especially birds. After it was banned worldwide in 1972, scientists believed it was the reason for the comeback of the bald eagle in the United States. Few people realized, therefore, that Genetically Modified Organism crops (GMO) and the sale of drugs were related to the pharmaceutical industry, which created a huge monopoly. The corporations aimed at making us sicker as time went by with expensive, quick fix solutions, and thus offering drugs to alleviate the symptoms. Many strange diseases and illnesses were showing up without explanation. With over-population, dwindling agricultural land and low food yields, the need for alternative hardy food sources became the motivation. Super seeds were created that would withstand drought, pests, poor soil conditions and cooler climates. Unfortunately, with that came the need to yield vast amounts of money through control of these new advancements.

***

Robert and Olena had been perplexed as to why their 8

year old daughter, Sophia, had unexplainable symptoms. Ever since she was born prematurely, they assumed it to be the cause for an array of illnesses yet to be diagnosed correctly by all the specialists. Living in Seattle, where the weather was damper than other parts of the country, they wondered if that very climate was affecting Sophia's immune system. In contrast, her 10 year old brother, Stephan, had fewer colds and flues. Nevertheless, he went through the all too frequent 'out of the blue' nosebleeds for unspecified reasons. Other than that, he was a healthy, robust boy who did relatively well in school and was interested in most sports. Head brimming with dark brown, curly hair, he was fairly muscular. He also possessed an inquisitive mind and a can-do attitude in all he set his mind to. Sophia was much more delicate than Stephan; even her skin was more porcelain-like with a body frame so willowy and thin stature to match. Her picturesque blue eyes, which always seemed at half-mast, belied her less than optimum health. Her hair, instead of being radiant and free-flowing, was dry and brittle and took on the appearance of a dirty blond tone. She was undoubtedly less daring in giving new things a go, and felt safer in familiar surroundings. On top of that, her condition left her drained and fatigued with no energy to spare. Her mind was always foggy, making it difficult to think clearly. Her eyesight, often blurred from double vision, kept her unsteady on her feet. In addition, rashes and sores covered a good portion of her arms and legs, keeping her awake at night when she needed sleep the most. No matter what her parents tried, they weren't able to alleviate her discomforts, and with that, felt helpless. With Sophia's fragile health, her parents had considered home schooling in the years ahead, with one of the parents needing to stay home.

Robert and Olena, both teachers, loved their summer holidays because they got to spend a good deal of time with their kids. Robert taught math in high school, which could be stressful now and then; Olena taught kindergarten. Both were fond of teaching. Robert was tall and more the quiet serious type, whereas Olena was very gregarious and would talk to anything that moved. She was very personable, as crows' feet around her eyes showed her sunny personality. A fresh scent of daily taken showers followed her throughout the day. Her students adored her and brought in little gifts on any occasion, thereby fulfilling her role as a teacher. They were like most North Americans, with all their inherent habits. Convenient, prepackaged lunches, bought at the grocers and quick fast food grabs, made up the larger part of their diet; given that the parents' time, when teaching, was in short supply. Every summer, the family looked forward to visiting Olena's parents in California, where they would stay for up to a month. Baba and Gido were both children's favorite relatives; since they got to be spoiled. Baba, meaning grandmother, and Gido, which meant grandfather, were from the old country of Ukraine. Baba was quite a large woman with a big laugh. She always wore her hair in a bun, and was not much into fashion, given that she wore the same simple outfits, year after year. She did possess great wisdom and could get that across with a certain look while remaining silent. You knew she meant it. Gido, on the other hand, was smaller and slimmer built, but one would never guess he was as strong as an ox. He religiously did his daily breakfast routine of raw, steel cut oats, with crushed flaxseed he prepared the night before, in order for the oats to be softened.

Both Baba and Gido did not believe in eating meals unless you prepared it yourself and were started from scratch. They, therefore, never ate at restaurants. They lived in suburbia on the edge of Garden Grove: a double lot with a vast, deep backyard not used for esthetic reasons, but rather for fruits and vegetables alone. Planted at the front of the house, however, were beautiful flower beds amidst the rock garden; but in the back, every square inch had been cultivated with edibles of all varieties. There were deeply trenched rows where huge vegetables grew, to sizes not seen commercially, to heavily laden fruit-bearing trees supported by many spindly sticks and posts. The variety of fruits and vegetables, created with companion planting, produced its own ecosystem. Various different companion vegetation that pests didn't like were planted in between the edibles; bugs and insects would not be found on them. Peppermint plants repelled ants, white cabbage moth, and beetles. Garlic discouraged fleas and Japanese beetles. Perennial Chives resisted aphids and spider mites, two very common garden pests. Chives were often planted among roses to keep aphids away, while Basil drove away flies and mosquitoes. Borage deterred the unpopular of vegetable garden insects, the tomato hornworm. Rosemary and Sage repelled cabbage moths, bean beetles, and carrot flies.

Annual Marigolds were used to deter Mexican bean beetles, squash bugs, tomato hornworms, and whiteflies. They were also known to repel harmful root knot nematodes (soil dwelling microscopic white worms) that attacked tomatoes, potatoes, roses, and strawberries. The root of the Marigold produced a chemical that killed nematodes as they entered the soil. Nasturtium, another annual, kept away the Colorado potato bugs and squash bugs.

This summer holiday, however, Sophia's health was weaker than usual and was barely able to muster up the enthusiasm to trek across two States. Her mother, Olena, was unsure if she should take this yearly journey, or to stay near their family doctor instead, in case of an emergency. Robert was required to stay home this year to teach summer school. Olena also vividly recalled how Sophia always returned home from her parents' place a brighter and happier daughter. She clearly never knew quite why, but figured it had to do with less stress and exposure to fresh air by being outdoors more. Baba and Gido didn't own a computer for the kids to spend hours on; they wouldn't know how to use one.

Olena and the kids decided to go anyway in hopes that this stay at the suburban farm would aid Sophia in some way. A list of telephone numbers from different hospitals en route was printed in case it was needed. They packed their usual convenient foods for the outing, with an occasional pit stop at some fast food joint. Sophia held on as best as she could and even bravely joined the family sing-alongs at the onset of their trip. The drive was long, but after having made this trip many times, it seemed to get shorter with each passing year. The overnight stay at a Motel for a short rest was somewhat effective in keeping the anticipation and liveliness up. It was hard for Sophia to stay awake, since she was still tired, but the thought of her grandparents kept her motivated.

"Are we there yet?" Sophia asked sleepily, awakened by the stop and go from the car, veering off the highway and onto streets; displaying flashing lights and stop signs.

"We're almost there, Soph, we're almost there," Stephan enthusiastically announced. Seeing as they were near their destination, he yelled, "Yeaaah!! We're here, we're finally here! Just a couple more blocks or so!" Stephan could hardly hold his excitement while clutching to his shoulder rest.

By the front door, Baba waited anxiously for their arrival, with Sophia and Stephan scuttling towards her as fast as they could. With a half-eaten hamburger concealed between crumpled wrappers in hand, Sophia offered it with elation to her grandmother.

"Here Baba, I saved it just for you."

Gracefully she replied, "Thank you, sweetheart, thank you. I'll save it for later."

With a concerned look at her daughter, Olena was aware her mother was, sooner or later, going to have a talk with her. She always did when it came to nutrition, and Olena always felt her mother was making too big a deal out of it. In any case, everyone they knew thought nothing of it and even believed she and the family ate healthier than most. After all, they kept the tomato and lettuce in their hamburgers.

In the backyard garden, Gido was plucking fruits and vegetables for canning and preserving. Stephan merrily hopped over for a greeting.

"Hi, Gido. I'm so glad to see you!" Stephan hollered while giving him a big bear hug and eagerly setting out to help him, an event he really enjoyed. He was busily munching on an apple, already picked. Again, as he always did, Gido reminded him of the same message:

"Stephan, you know it is important to eat good. It'll make you strong like bull. And you know Baba and Gido never get sick," he told him. Stephan looked puzzled. To Stephan, somehow, the fruit always tasted better than the produce his mother bought from the store.

Inside, Baba and Olena were already preparing dinner with the wholesome harvest Gido had collected. Baba and Gido, already getting on with age, showed remarkable endurance and physical strength to keep up with their gardening. Their lives were lived around routine and discipline and an "early to bed and early to rise" philosophy. There was little to complain about.

After their full bellies were finished off with a home baked apple pie, Sophie and Stephan were dead beat from the day's excursions and were contently ready for bed. That evening, Olena's parents worriedly disclosed to her how their edible garden has suffered numerous attempts at being sabotaged. Garbage had been thrown into the highly fenced-off garden; a fence they thought would keep their land protected, since it was next to a walking path. Even bugs and garden pests, mysteriously thrown over the fence into their wholesome garden, were being somehow used to destroy their bountiful crop. Olena's parents would never exploit such a thing, since they couldn't imagine doing it to someone else. They didn't understand the reasoning behind it.

"Olena," her mother queried. "There were two men

who came by. They said they worked for the agricultural department... and said they had these new seeds, which would be much better than the ones we've always used. They also said, that... we would never have any problems with them... because they were specially made and we would never have to worry if we forget about watering the plants... or... or... if there were no nutrients left in the soil... the plants would still grow. I was scared because they were being really pushy, and tried to force me to buy them. I told them that we were happy the way we had been growing our own food, and that we have no worries. We know where the seeds came from and we know the seeds were organic with no problems, ever. We always knew it was safe to eat them. How did we know if the new seeds could promise us the same guarantee? My answer was simple."

"What did you end up doing, mom?" Olena asked with trepidation. "Did you actually buy some?"

The mother shook her head. "Why should I? My seeds have done well all along. I don't need them." She paused for a moment and added, "Anyways, have you heard that there are private investigators who spy on farms...and seed dealers... and co-ops? And did you know that...when you buy their seeds, they make you sign an agreement so you can't use the seeds from the plants for re-planting and re-selling? There are even rumors going around that the seeds they make can't even reproduce themselves... so... so that you have to buy the seeds from them every year!"

Ever since these new seeds have been used for agriculture, strange health issues with people in town were showing up.

"Here we don't get sick. Everything we eat is not poisoned with chemicals 'cause we don't use pesticides." She paused yet another moment. "Olena, do you maybe think that Sophia could be having these weird health problems because of the food you feed her? Do you not see that every time Sophia visits, she feels so much better? Stephan too... he doesn't have any nosebleeds. Why should I, then, give up my seeds for the ones they offer me?"

For the first time, Olena pondered her mother's questioning, and seriously considered it, for there might be truth to her words regarding her daughter's health. In the days ahead, she took note that in the brief time they were there, Sophia's health was on the path to convalescence. Even her cheeks displayed a rosy glow, as well as a sparkle of vivacity in her eyes, not seen while they were at home.

With continued harassment from the two men who wanted Baba to give up her seeds, in exchange for theirs, Olena decided she had to do something. Apprehensive for her parents lives, Olena set out to find answers and visited the local library where she could use the computer and do an internet search. She came across article after article; could this be what her mother was warning her about? She read how genetically modified foods were cause for panic due to risk of horizontal gene transfer. Might this be what her mother was facing? A possibility. But why her? She didn't have a farm. Baba did have one of the most luscious gardens she'd ever seen, and this would put most other gardens to shame.

Apparently, genetically modified foods were referred to as "Frankenstein Foods", and had now found their way into the food chain and to our dinner table without our knowing. Was this maybe what Sophia's unexplained symptoms were related to? She questioned in her mind about this infliction, this strange disease; she thought at first it was merely science fiction, since it gave the impression of being far-fetched. People with this condition explained it as parasitic bugs crawling beneath their skin, showing slow-to-heal open sores with plastic string-like fibers oozing out. Fibers so strong when you pulled on them, they created searing pain. This was a pain so unbearable; people had been known to commit suicide over it since doctors didn't know what to do. It could only be explained as imaginary symptoms, because the doctors found it so implausible they couldn't believe it entirely. This unexplained skin condition may have had ties with our, so-called new foods, generating havoc with our DNA by genetically modifying the genes and, thus, altering the species barrier.

Over the next several days, the men who visited previously were persistently harassing and threatening Olena's parents. They would lie to them by telling them that their superior seeds would eventually destroy their organic seeds through cross-pollination and would ultimately render them useless. Refusing to listen, Baba and Gido ignored their sales pitch. In the meantime, they had gathered many seeds of all varieties and had secretly packaged them so they could be sent oversees to their relatives in the Ukraine and others abroad. A pact was made and an underground secrecy was established to keep the unadulterated seeds alive and well, in order for these organic seeds to be kept from complete annihilation. Each of their relatives would do the same and would send out clean seeds to all whom they knew.

But in the days ahead, however, when waking up one morning, they found their garden completely demolished and uprooted, exposing gaping holes in their well-protected fence. Row by row, all the vegetables were turned over, with roots sticking up looking dried up and wilted. It was a point of no return for them, for sure. All the prized fruit, which bore the symbol of years of knowledge and hard work, were wiped out in an instant. A sticky gooey substance had the appearance of liquid tar, covered all the fruit on all the trees and rendered them inedible.

Their instincts paid off as they were prepared for the worst case scenario as it turned out to be. Luckily, hundreds of jars from saving their preserves would allow them to still live off of their land for years to come. What were they to do? With their garden shed door broken into, they found all contents strewn about. Was this a burglary? Or was everything only revolving around the seeds? Knowing Baba and Gido saved their seeds in a special hide out, they'd pretended to leave out seeds for planting, intentionally, for the investigators to find by making it seem like they were meant to be hidden. Since they wanted common peace restored in their lives, they decided to go along and buy the hybrid seeds. They would falsely promise to use them the following year by signing a contract, and even willingly asked them to be sure they could buy the seeds from them again the following years. They went as far as to show, as if they held great interest in the new found seeds, just to get the seed police off their back, knowing full well they would replace them with their very own. After all, how could they differentiate between the two seeds, since they grew their own pest-free organic greens; just as long as they were being cooperative.

Now convinced, Olena embraced the idea that Sophia may have been suffering from this modern food syndrome, and all the processed food the family had been ingesting all these years. As a schoolteacher, with a love for knowledge and learning, how could she not have figured this out? Were she and Robert that busy? Didn't either have the time or frame of mind for this kind of awareness? How about all their friends and colleagues? Were they in the dark, too? Had any one of them ever questioned the food and produce they bought from stores without knowing the source behind it? How was it that no one was ever informed on this hugely important information? After all, it affected everyone's health. Was it all a secret? Did all of them plainly accept it, just because the government and the Food and Drug Administration regulators said it was okay? What other truths behind scientific data was kept from them? She vowed to become a 'save the seed' crusader when she got back by sharing her story with others willing to open their minds.

Reaching out towards her mom by hugging her, at long last, it made sense to her. "I'm just horrified!" she exclaimed.

"I've been poisoning my children with convenience foods." Olena's hug was tighter than usual, gripped with thankfulness and gratitude.

"Do you understand now? Do you finally get what I've been telling you all this time? We fed you with the food grown in our yard, and you were rarely sick. There was a reason for that. Little nutrition is in the new seeds... and they are no good for you."

Hope was renewed within the family when Olena vowed to change their eating habits when they returned home, to Seattle. Gradually noticeable improvements took form in Sophia's overall health, including a more balanced weight gain, combined with lustrous hair and colorful skin tone. Her eyes, too, had a sparkle rarely ever seen prior to now. She was almost a different person from before, with bountiful energy. She no longer missed schooldays. Extensive and boring doctor and hospital visits became a thing of the past. How she dreaded them. Stephan, with school grades at an all time best, no longer had those embarrassing nosebleeds, especially in class. When playing sports, his maneuvering on the field was faster and quicker, and he proved himself a valuable team player, with his teammates vying for him to be on their team. Olena now only shopped at organic food outlets, keeping in mind the important PLU code—five digits preceded by the number nine—that set healthy and modified foods apart. She and Robert had noted better health overall and hadn't realized the constant sniffles had stopped also. Both enjoyed more vitality and endurance and found teaching less draining than previously experienced. Olena no longer abides to the standard North American fast food diets, if her life and that of her family, depended on it.

THE SINGING LARK
JOSEPHINE APPENG

HE stood uneasily in front of the door, the number seventeen neatly imprinted on a plaque in the centre. His watch showed quarter to ten and he was a few minutes early. The infirmary area had few people, but he liked it that way. It was a dazzling clear day, although the mornings were as bitter cold as winter. Numerous cumulus clouds adorned the sky. A swift breeze whipped up his long overcoat, and his thick but loose dark brown hair fluttered across his chestnut coloured eyes. Breathing in the crisp cool air, Miguel turned the knob and entered. The small white room looked hollow and lonely. A bed was placed against the right wall with a tiny night table partnered alongside it. The girl was already sitting upright in her collared cotton pyjamas and her attention was fixed outside the narrow curved window. The girl had slender, high cheekbones, a thin frame and vivid eyes. Upon his arrival she glanced up at the young man and smiled. "You didn't have to come, you know."

Miguel removed his overcoat, "Isn't it my responsibility to check up on you every now and then?"

She frowned, "I don't want to be a bother, since you're already so busy."

Miguel gave a short laugh and sat beside her, "That's not going to stop me. You need all the support you can get, Yuna." He tousled her long delicate brown hair.

She faintly scowled. "Tell me about work. Are there as many patients as before?"

"No. Although I'm not the doctor they still get me to do a lot, like check up on you," he reached for a clipboard and examined the intricate data. She giggled at his analytic, yet charming face. They spent the rest of the afternoon playing card games and flipping through pictured books. They talked and laughed together. Her intoxicating smile matched up with his wholehearted disposition. For a moment, the silence, which had fallen between the two, was inscrutable, but both were undeniably happy of each other's company.

"I want to go outside..." she softly spoke. Her peaceful face masked a bursting aspiration.

"You're improving, but you won't be able to handle the air just yet."

"It's a beautiful day." She sat up on her knees and peered out the window. "I want to see the sky."

"Don't worry, you will," Miguel heartened. "You will."

Miguel hurried down the air corridor, but paused to admire the remaining glow of orange that was retreating into the distance. Its unknown destination seemed like the end of the world. It was an odd sentiment. The rapid air train flickered under the metropolitan lights and could be seen approaching the deck. As it slowed to a hiss, Miguel stared up. He felt miniature compared to the towering, silver structures surrounding him. This world that he had known all his life remained dominant, glassy and flowing, sophisticated in all aspects. He stood near the large tinted windows watching the illuminate buildings flash by. The city functioned flawlessly and public infringement rarely happened. Human beings worked and lived their lives out in this utopia without concern. No foreign policy could breach the safety measures. Health care was universal and the centered significance in society. Everything around him was a product of progression and would continue to improve. The train he occupied was an empty, silent but powerful entity cruising throughout the city. The flicker of buildings suddenly stopped. Replaced before him was the endless expanse of the night sky. Miguel's face lightened the instant; a pint-sized golden glow caught his eye. A fair amount of it had filled the twilight past the glass.

This was Karium, the element that fuelled the advanced city; without it, life could not sustain. In its natural state, Karium is like a visible, spherical gas, but like electricity, it can be harnessed for power. This element, produced from the atmosphere's ionization, enables the city to hover within the atmosphere. Scientists have also been able to use its composition as an aid for medicinal use by doctors. No one knew where this spectacle had materialized and wondered whether it had always been here and if not, did life even occur prior to this?

A light shower of rain began to fall and polish the city as soon as he stepped off the train. The *World Archives* building was a familiar place to visit; Miguel settled himself at his usual spot and indulged in a thick volume he had started to read a while back.

At the present era of development from fuel-efficient hybrid cars to five-year floating aircrafts the progress on environmental issues has been lengthy. Health problems have swelled dramatically due to the increase of anthropogenic waste, in particular the emission of greenhouse gases. This crucial matter has reached its greatest magnitude and in spite of most efforts to recede the multiplying consequences, it was not enough to completely transpose the damage. Over the years, the elimination of diseases such as malaria has grounded to a halt because of high temperatures. Furthermore, extreme and unbalanced weather conditions have proved to be an effect of global warming, and drastically influences global economies. In terms of health, the casualties of humans occur at a more constant rate from respiratory problems and many other concerns.

Miguel broke from his concentration. Reading this article was like watching the sequences of events in an entirely different world. He pushed back into his seat and breathed. This account had been at least a millennium ago. How much had this world really changed?

The next day was even frigid, signalling winter's arrival. Thankfully, the visit to Yuna's helped him ease his way through the day.

"I saw an odd bird flying in the sky alone this morning. It had a light coloured underside and dark stripes on top. It was singing something nice," she mentioned blithely.

"It must have been a lark. There aren't many around. You

were lucky to see it." Earlier, Miguel had spoken with her doctor and learned that she would soon be discharged. Yuna was born with weak lungs and respiratory troubles but having given new treatments with sources extracted from Karium, she was recovering at a great rate.

"I want to see it again. The lark."

"You will. I'll show it to you," he smiled warmly.

"So, did you learn anything new?" she murmured in a low voice.

Miguel tried to look relaxed, "What are you talking about?"

"Don't try to hide it, I can tell. You went to the Archives last night!"

He sighed and passed her an earnest look, "I saw them. The lights." Miguel keenly described his observations from the night before: the enchanting twilight sky, the beautiful fields of shimmering gold, Karium drifting in gentle euphoria, and his discoveries at the Archives. Yuna was filled with wonder and she remarked how eager she would be the moment of her release.

The following morning, Miguel decided to return to his area of the infirmary. He found a group of men wearing dark suits in the wing, conversing with the doctor. They were members of the government health agency who had come to assess the Karium treatment.

"Frankly, this data is insufficient. Your progress is lacking pace," one of the men, a stocky one, declared. "Your patients need to be given a greater quantity; otherwise the process would be too long and slow. They'll be in here forever!"

Incredulity was etched on the doctor's weary face. "Isn't that a bit hasty? Our patients are doing very well and I don't see any problems with the amount we're administering. I mean, how and where could we get more—"

A slimmer man cut him short, "That's why we're here." He drew out a document with a photo clipped on. "Our new invention will generate enough energy to power the city for centuries ahead of us and offer enough dosage for current and future patients. Fortunately for you, we're having a showing of this gizmo half an hour from now so you'll get a chance to see what we're talking about. " The doctor was clearly discombobulated.

"Pardon me, but is there something wrong, Dr. Foehn?" The members in dark suits shot puzzled looks at Miguel's advance.

"Yes well, I suppose we'll just have to go and take a look at it." He gestured for Miguel.

Then the stocky man stepped forward, "I'm sorry but the viewing is for only authorized personnel."

"He's my assistant, he'll come or I will not." Foehn firmly stated.

The trip had been tense; the air was thick and neither had spoken. The warm, rich sunlight flooded through the windows into the train's interior, but the men seemed to have withdrawn into the shadows.

"Sir, is it really alright for me to come?" Miguel whispered.

"I don't see why not. Anyway, it may be good for you to know," the doctor quietly replied. The men led them through a hallway towards a large atrium. The hub was at a sky scraping level, overlooking the metropolis. Black and white, checker-pattern tiles covered the floor, and the walls were tall glass windows. Placed in the middle was an enormous metallic-yellow mechanism. The curvature of it was evident from the top of the crown, to the arcing cylinders that connected somewhere. A central core was embedded on the front surface and the whole contraption emanated a drone.

"As you can see, this device is designed to run 100% error-free. It's well-engineered, long lasting and produces up to 100 Karowatt per second," said the stocky man. "We'll have it running tomorrow morning," he proudly added.

Miguel was alarmed; what would all of this mean? "Wait, it sounds like you're sucking up a lot of Karium. Wouldn't that make the atmosphere unbalanced?"

Another man, with deep sunken eyes, had spoken up for the first time, "I admit that it's a bold step but we assure you, the consistent ionization within the thermosphere will make up for it." He was less stern than the other, more executive men. The nametag on his blazer read Mr. Charleston.

Still uncertain, Miguel said, "You can't do this. It's not going to work."

"A youth, like you, would find it hard to understand," the slimmer man smirked.

Miguel's voice had risen, "Shut up! You don't get it! People are going to get hurt once you've consumed all the Karium!" He had a sudden sensation of encountering a similar scenario. Turning on his heels, Miguel headed straight for the exit. As soon as he stepped outside, he broke into a dash. Thoughts ran through his mind and the farther he distanced himself from that building, the more anxious he became. He remembered the image of the gold Karium from that night, and Yuna. Their man-made machine could make the air almost impossible to breathe, especially for the sensitive people.

He reached the infirmary and made his way for Yuna's floor; she would be released the next day. He veered the corner and what came into view startled him. Standing on the air corridor, she peered over the edge and gazed out towards the sky. Miguel called her name and she looked over and asked, "Where have you been?"

"What are you doing out here?" Miguel grasped her shoulders with both hands. "You can't stand outside! C'mon let's go in." He was about to lead her off but she wrenched her arm away.

"No, I'm fine and I don't have to go in. Tell me what you were doing first."

"How long have you been out here?"

"Maybe half an hour. But why? What's wrong?" Half an hour wasn't bad, Miguel thought. He sighed in relief and turned to the sky. She was reckless, but he couldn't blame her; being out in the open was like a refreshing taste of freedom.

"Were you looking for it? The lark?" he asked. There was no response and he looked back at her. Panic struck as he realized, Yuna was kneeling over and wheezing desperately.

That evening, Miguel was leaning against the wall waiting. She had been transferred to an inner room of the infirmary, and he hadn't heard from her since. He felt exhausted from the constant pang of guilt and he asked himself, how could this have happened? It was entirely his fault. A moment later Dr. Foehn appeared and said that she hadn't received her morning treatment and if Yuna had stayed out there any longer it may have been critical. Yuna needed to recover and her release would be postponed.

The doctor smiled and patted his shoulder, "She'll be fine. We all make mistakes. This wasn't yours."

Then Miguel remembered. "The generator. Will they really launch it tomorrow?"

The doctor breathed, "I'm afraid it's definite and I'm worried about the possible side effects." Miguel felt the same and as he retired for the night, his mind was a treadmill.

Miguel's head throbbed and sleep was out of the question. He noticed the sky was dim grey as he strolled down the air corridor and reflected upon the events. That machine would start running today and luckily, Yuna's release was delayed, but how would she feel? He wondered how they would cope with these many changes. "I just want things to be normal," he said to himself before knocking on her door. Miguel carefully entered and was surprised to find her awake and expecting him. He could see Yuna had lost colour and appeared frail. The respirator hung loosely beside her.

"How are you doing, Yuna?"

"You're the doctor. You tell me," she calmly uttered.

"I'm not a doctor remember?" He pulled up a chair next to her and smiled, "But I'll tell you that you'll be fine." Yuna did not laugh nor smile back but rather, held a melancholic expression. He fidgeted in his chair.

"Have I been selfish?" she asked.

"Of course not. Don't say that." Then he pressed her head against his shoulder. "Cheer up. You'll be able to go outside again in about a week."

She pushed away, "A week! Miguel, I don't want to stay here anymore!"

"But you need to recuperate –"

"I'm alright now! I saw it, the sky, for real! Please don't take this chance away from me!" she cried in a shaky voice.

"I'm very sorry. I promise though, that you will see it."

One night, Miguel was on his way to the Archives. The air felt unusual when he boarded the train, but he was quite bothered when he realized the field of glowing lights that previously flourished the rural sky, had completely disappeared. At the infirmary, the staffs were busier than usual and a there was a slight increase in admission. People came in coughing, some bleakly waited with respirators on their mouths, and others sat, seeming to fluctuate between consciousnesses. Every now and then, cases of harvested Karium came in masses through the swinging double doors. The visits have been somber and Yuna spent most of her time lying in bed. Her condition didn't appear to be improving at all.

At once, he left the infirmary running along the dark deserted roads and crossed the decks. Aboard the silent train, he felt as if the world outside was quivering. Miguel hurried towards the central building he had visited with the doctor. In the lobby, he was immediately stopped by an official and denied entry to the Karium generator. "You don't understand! That thing must be shut off! Lives are at stake!" He struggled with the persistent official, until he spotted a group of suited men walking down the hall; one had deep sunken eyes. "Mr.

Charleston!" he called. The executives looked his way and Miguel rushed towards them leaving the irritated guard behind. "Mr. Charleston, you have to shut off the Karium generator, please! It's a huge mistake!"

The stocky man moved forward, "Listen, boy, you're the huge mistake. You've got nerve coming here but you're just wasting your time. We're not shutting anything off."

"But you can't imagine the suffering it's causing! The air will become unstable and things will fall apart," Miguel showed them the thick book from the Archives that he had been carrying. "Look, Earth became unsustainable because humans polluted the air. What you're doing with that generator is taking away the necessity to breathe. You're practically following the footsteps of the 21st century!"

"This is outrageous, where'd you get this…so-called evidence from? You know kid, you're really taking up my time and I'm getting pissed off." The stocky man struck the book sending it across the floor. In resentment, Miguel advanced, but the official suddenly approached, grabbed his arm and started to drag him away.

"Let go of me!" he exclaimed, as he was taken further from his last hope. "People will die! Mr. Charleston, please I'm begging you!!" For a second, the sunken-eyed man regretfully watched him disappear from sight.

He had been defeated. Fate brought him back to the infirmary as he walked down the air corridor under the foreboding sky. What else could he do? He knew the machine was absorbing way too much for the atmosphere to produce. The situation would worsen and by then it may be too late, he thought. Somehow, he had to inform the federal government before lives could be lost. A dim figure stood alone near the railing. His eyes widen and his hands froze.

"Yuna!" He ran to her side. "Why are you out here?" She remained silent. A gust picked up and wobbled her stance. Miguel caught her and realized Yuna's body was limp and icy.

Her lost expression stared out ahead at the dusky grey sky. "Yuna please, get up! Snap out of it!" he cried in a distraught voice. He shook her and Yuna lifted her arm and pointed into the distance. A distinct melody sounded through the gentle sprinkle of white snowflakes, which began to fall across this troubled city.

"Miguel, look." She quietly muttered, "A lark." Indeed, a single lark was gliding among the clouds, singing its song as it slowly faded away. She watched the snow waft and asked, "Is that Karium?"

He hesitated but then replied, "Yes." Yuna smiled and closed her eyes. She puffed a white cloud of breath and all became silent. There were no Karium lights around but he felt as if a bright, warm glow had drifted away from him. Miguel hugged her; his face felt hot and his vision blurred. Whatever happened, they would be together. Deep in the city, the generator proceeded to hum but Miguel wouldn't leave; he didn't want to leave.

TRACKER
DYLAN COLLIER

The morning crowd wasn't too talkative. Many sat alone in their booths eating either the fried eggs and bacon on toast or the stack of waffles doused in syrup. This caused Sam's Diner to be relatively quiet; the faint scraping of utensils, the slight sipping of orange juice or coffee, and the muffled dialogue from the television were the only substantial noises inside. The television was hanging on the wall in the corner. Most of the people sitting across the front metal counter were watching, not with intent, but because it was there. Sam brought over a small cup and plate to a man who just sat down, and began pouring coffee.

"Cream and sugar?" Sam asked the man.

"No thank you," the man replied. He wore a light grey hooded-sweatshirt, with the hood up so no one could see his face, an old pair of jeans that were slightly frayed around the bottoms and knees, and sneakers that also looked quite old and tattered. He lifted his hood back so he could look Sam in the eye. He looked at Sam, and Sam looked back. The man had eyes that were an ashen grey; in the glare of the light they showed a speckle of hazel. The man's face looked as if it had been unshaven for a few days; his stubble covered jaw was fairly pronounced and gave him a rigid look. His hair was medium length, a dark brown color, and was also in a chaotic state. He looked at his left wrist as he pulled up his sleeve, revealing a finely made black watch; it was 8:30 AM. Sam noticed that the expensive looking watch seemed to be out of place with the rest of his physical characteristics.

"Would you mind turning up the TV, please?" His voice was scratchy and rough but he had a very pristine way of speaking, his words seemed to flow as if they were written.

"Sure, I don't see why not." Sam answered with a Boston accent. He pulled the remote out from under the counter and turned it up a few notches. The television was still not loud enough, but the words were now comprehensible. It was channel 26, WWNN, the World Wide News Network, the theme music began playing as the headline read "WWNN Special Report: Asclepius Friend or Foe?"

"Good morning viewers, I am Leonardo Rousseau and this is a WWNN special news report." A blond haired man in a respectable brown suit began to speak with an enthusiastic tone. "I'm here today to ask and inform you, the general public, about the medical company Asclepius. As many of you know, this company has brought about many great medical discoveries and cures for several previously thought incurable diseases, but it also has brought us to our current state. I have much reason to believe that this company is the reason the whole world is now being watched and controlled by the seven that call themselves The Theorists." The blond man seemed to be getting worked up by this story; he raised his voice and had replaced his comforting enthusiastic tone with a cynical, hate-filled one. "Before I get ahead of myself, let's be clear I have no physical proof of this, but if you carefully look at the evidence I will bring to the table, it seems to all add up as a giant conspiracy plot between The Theorists and Asclepius." Leonardo calmed his voice and took a sip from his coffee cup. "Alrighty, I'll start with Asclepius's beginnings. It was first established in 2022 near the west coast in Canada, in British Columbia. However, the founder was never named or even publicly shown in the media. This seems suspicious if you ask me. This company quickly rose to the number one medical research facility in North America. Is this a coincidence that the Theorists are currently using that first Asclepius research facility as their headquarters?" Leonardo sipped his coffee once again as he stared into the camera with his eyebrows raised. "And every person in North America bought their products and supported Asclepius. This profit wave made them wealthier than several software companies combined, which at the time meant that Asclepius was the richest company in North America. A year later they expanded, and Asclepius International was born. The research company was brought to the other continents. Thus, Asclepius became the most prosperous company in history. With this amount of resources, Asclepius was the perfect company for the Theorists to use as a cover." Yet another sip followed, this time a small sigh was expelled afterwards. "At the beginning of the New Year, the UN passed a law where all criminals are to be implanted, via injection, synthetic blood infused with nanotechnology GPS trackers inside. Who would have guessed that this crime reducing technology would soon be in all of us? Anyway, by mid-2024, Asclepius had created a vaccine for the Ebola virus, a deadly disease that kills ninety percent of the people it comes in contact with. At the time this was a fantastic discovery." This time Leonardo took a much longer drink from his cup. He cleared his throat and continued, "Soon after a grand majority of people were vaccinated, studios worldwide received an anonymous report that within the vaccine was the same tracker that had been placed inside criminals. As you may recall, the next day seven blackened out figures took control of every television station and affirmed that they were the ones who did this. They also stated that the head of Asclepius, who yet again remained unnamed, had handed the company over to them. They called themselves the Theorists. With their wealth and the tracking system, they brought about a new world order with themselves as our leaders. Another report was leaked to the press. It stated that using the tracking system the Theorists were blackmailing many world leaders as well as high ranking people inside the UN. This blackmail enabled them to take control of the major countries of the world. When they established control they gained even more fortune, and with this money they purchased more companies for their personal gain. Today, the Theorists own the majority of companies, giving them almost unlimited power. They leave the press alone, because they believe in free speech, but how long can that last? Power is an addicting drug, and it's only a matter of time before they even control our thoughts. This leads me to believe that they were behind Asclepius the whole time. Whilst initial intentions were good, this road that they went down is morally despicable, and I for one-" The diner listeners were interrupted by a slamming of the door, the man in the light grey hooded sweater was gone. He had left a few dollars by his finished coffee.

The streets were busy; most people were walking, buses and a few cars crowded the roads, others were riding their newly developed hover boards powered by high strength magnets. "Watch where you're going!" A young boy shouted at the man in the light grey sweater. He didn't feel the need to respond and just continued walking, determined to get somewhere.

He eventually found his way to a deserted building and took out his cell phone. He dialed a number with an unwavering look upon his face. "Kaleb, it's time." He paused as he listened to Kaleb on the other end.

"Jack, why now?" Kaleb answered in a hesitant tone.

"Don't ask, I've already sent you my part and paid you. Generously, I might add. Just send the complete file to my phone." Jack hung up the phone with a small beep. He chuckled slightly, "Kaleb, who thought that we'd be finishing this?" he mused to himself. After he spoke Jack let out a louder laugh. Jack's phone beeped once again, and he looked at it. The front read file transfer complete. He smiled and walked on. Jack eventually made his way to the train station nearby; he walked through the scanner. Based off the tracker, it showed who he was, his vital signs, as well as all of his background information to the security team. They let Jack through with ease. He paid for a cross country ticket to British Columbia. He boarded the train, and took a seat beside the window. Rain began to trickle down the glass as he stared into the darkening sky. He fell into the dark abyss of his dreams.

"Sir. Sir? We're here." A young woman in a red uniform

patted Jack on the shoulder.

Jack opened his eyes, and stared at the woman in front of him. He blinked twice. He was still in a dazed state. "T-Thank you, Miss Thompson," he replied, finding her name on a golden nametag. He got to his feet and exited the train along with the other passengers. He followed the crowd through the airport-like terminal. Jack finally reached the security terminal. Standard procedure; people in front of him seemed to be going through very quickly. It was Jack's turn; he stepped through the arch and took two more steps before he was stopped.

"Mr. Bolton? Are you alright?" A man in a black uniform asked Jack, with a concerned look on his face.

Jack turned to meet the man's eyes. "Yes, I'm fine, why do you ask?"

"Well, the scanner shows your vitals, and apparently you're having a cardiac arrest." The man replied, squinting at the screen. "It's probably just a malfunction but could you go through again, just to make sure that you don't need medical attention."

"Uh, sure." Jack looked at his watch, and then at the clock near the security desk. His watch was 4 hours ahead. He looked closer at his watch, the second hand was moving at irregular intervals, very fast, then stopping suddenly. Jack stared back at the man and focused, thinking about his next move. Another guard moved closer to make sure there was no trouble. Jack decided to run. He ran harder than he had in his entire life. It took a few seconds for the guards to comprehend what was happening, but as soon as they grasped the situation they began their pursuit. They shouted for backup as well as for Jack to stop. Jack slipped through the crowds giving slight pushes when he needed to get through. The guards were gaining on him as he exited the building.

Outside the sun shined. The streets here were also crowded with the same kinds of people as back in Toronto.

Tall buildings filled the cityscape. They were all a white or a light shade of grey, and the windows were all tinted black. The noise of the city was immense; it drowned out the shouts from his pursuers.

Jack got an idea. As he ran along the sidewalk he pulled out some money from his pocket. He grabbed a young man off his hover board and threw the money at him as he took the board. Jack jumped on the board, and quickly gained balance on the unstable vehicle. Jack lunged forward and sped off down the sidewalk, dodging the public; he turned down an alleyway and jumped over some boxes of trash. He began to hum "The Power of Love" by Huey Lewis and the News as he rode. Jack heard sirens from several streets around him, and he decided to stick to the alleys. He continued until he couldn't hear the sirens anymore and jumped off the board.

Suddenly Jack's arms were grabbed and pushed behind him. He was quick to respond and managed to pull one of his arms away. He turned to face his captor. It was a woman; she was dressed in a black police uniform, her light brown hair shimmered in the sunlight, and her dark green eyes stared into his as her grip tightened. She smiled and twisted his arm, forcing him to one knee. Jack growled in pain as he fell. "So you're the guy that everyone's looking for?" The woman asked with a light hearted tone.

Jack grunted, "And it seems you're the one who caught me." He pulled forward and turned his body, bringing him to his feet with one free hand, staring at the woman again. "You're quite beautiful, you know?" he smiled and tilted his head.

"You're not bad yourself." She tried to flip him but he grabbed her wrist and stopped her. "And you can fight, not bad. It's a shame you have to go to jail." She kicked him in the stomach and he dropped to his knees. She quickly pulled out her handcuffs.

"Wait! Don't do this," he looked up at her, squinting in

pain. "You have to let me go."

"And why on earth would I let you go? Catching you is going to get me promoted." She laughed at the end of her sentence.

"Because I'm going to take down the Theorists." Jack replied

"Ha, you? And why would I ever believe that?" She responded with a sarcastic tone.

"Seriously! You have to let me go. Haven't you ever wanted to be free? Do you trust me?" Jack's voice was flooding with desperation as well as sincerity as he was on his knees.

She looked at him. Her eyes met his and she understood what she had to do. She loosened her grip, eventually letting go, and took a step backwards. "The Theorists killed my parents because they stood out against them. If you can take them down, then I do trust you. As I have been informed your name is Jack Bolton. My name's Alicia Hawthorn, I don't know why, but I trust you, Jack." She spoke as if his words touched her deepest sympathy. Jack was smiling, Alicia didn't know why, so she inquired. "Why are you smiling like that?" She grasped his arms again, this time tighter in case it was a trap.

He chuckled, "Since we're being so trusting, I should tell you that my name isn't Jack. While the tracker in me does say that is my name, it isn't." He stood to his feet and stared back into her eyes.

"Well," she paused. "What is your name? And how did you manage to trick the tracker?" She asked her brows furrowed in curiosity and confusion.

"Ha, I'm sorry, there's no one who knows my real name... aside from an old acquaintance or two. If you let me go I will tell you how I duped the tracker." He raised one eyebrow and looked at her hands clenched tightly against his forearms. She released him but watched him closely, for she wanted to know his secret, and in case he ran. "Thanks. Well what I did was taped raw steaks to my arms and attached a synthetic skin over top. While it looked like I was really ripped, I was planning. When they injected me with the vaccine, it went directly into the meat and not my arm. They scanned to see if the tracker worked properly and it did because it was inside the steak. I then went home and took out the tracker and rigged it to my watch," He lifted his sleeve and showed her the watch. "This is a how I get through the clearances without being identified as dead. It keeps time for my vitals, like an artificial heartbeat. Unfortunately my watch has recently malfunctioned, and that's why it looked like I was having a cardiac arrest. I also altered the information and that was that. From that day on I was Jack Bolton." He finished his story with a smirk of accomplishment on his lips.

"How- How did you know that they were planting a tracker inside?" She asked.

"Ahh, you're a smart young lady. That is not important at this time. I have to leave, I've said too much. Please, don't follow me." He turned to leave, but was stopped by her hand once again grabbing his arm. "Do you trust me?" he asked. She nodded and let him go; he broke into a jog and then hopped back on his hover board. He was off, avoiding trash and other boxes that were blocking his path, gracefully weaving through the alleyways.

Jack wandered aimlessly for a while through the unfamiliar surroundings; he hadn't been in Vancouver for quite some time. Jack was in an old run down industrial section. It was to be renovated within the year and replaced with new apartments and stores. He finally reached an abandoned warehouse that he recognized. Jack looked around the outside, for the doors were locked. He stumbled upon an old rusted oil drum; he pushed it over and grabbed a shiny silver key from the imprint the drum had left. "Ha, I'm surprised your still here." Jack mused to himself staring at the key. He unlocked the door, walked in, and flipped a switch to his right. One light lit in the centre of the room, it illuminated a small wooden desk. Jack walked over to it and sat down in a dusty leather chair. Upon the desk were a laptop and some small tools. He opened the laptop and it turned on, and he began to work. He was reprogramming his tracker; he changed his name to Anthony Kidman. He also took apart his watch and fixed the gear that caused the problem before. "Finally I'm done," he sighed. "Tomorrow it ends." He grabbed a small blanket from under his chair and curled up and fell asleep for the night.

Jack was awakened by the sun shining through a window near the top of the building. He got out of his chair and stretched out his muscles with a robust yawn. He walked over to a metal cabinet on the right wall. Jack opened it to reveal a black suit and a red tie. He smiled and replaced his clothes with these new ones. He looked like a professional and was proud of it. He put his watch on and put his cell phone in his right jacket pocket. He walked to his hover board and grabbed it. He rode out of the building and sped off towards Asclepius's main facility. Jack looked quite unfitting in his new clothes while on the hover board that is designed for young adults or teenagers, but he didn't care about the frequent stares. Finally, he was within sight of the main building, after winding along the sidewalks and avoiding the walking traffic.

Jack jumped off his board and threw it into a nearby dumpster. He walked to the front of the building. Jack built his confidence by breathing calmly and steadily, for he knew he was about to free the world. He walked in, the doors opened automatically; as he stepped into the building he found it oddly relaxing to be in the lion's den. Jack looked around himself and checked his watch inconspicuously. What he saw was a lobby to a very busy research facility, many white lab coats were walking by him in a blind hurry. Before he was allowed into the main lobby he was scanned for his tracker, and this time it went smoothly. There were five cameras pointed in various locations so that there would be no blind spots. To avoid detection he looked at his watch when a camera turned towards him. Jack knew the layout of the building fairly well, he managed to hack into the city's mainframe and find blueprints for reference. He headed to the stairs; knowing that elevators were a trap in this kind of situation. When he opened the door Jack looked up to check for any other people. There was no one, so he began to climb. Each time he reached a floor he peered into the windows for the Theorist's main computer. Jack stopped his search when he reached the second highest floor.

Inside the room it was very dark, only lit by a few small blinking lights. He did not see any people in the room, so he slowly attempted to push the door. It didn't budge, so Jack jiggled the handle. "Damn," He noticed that beside the door was a keypad with a fingerprint lock. "There's always a way around computers." Jack pulled out his phone and a small cord out of his pocket. He plugged one end of the cord into the keypad and the other end into his phone. Jack clicked several buttons on his phone; he was quite quick with any kind of electronic. He then placed his thumb on the keypad, a little light went green and the door slid open. Jack walked into the dark room.

The whirring of the computers was fairly loud. The server towers were as tall as he was. Many wires were strewn across the floor all connecting to one massive computer. It was black and had a big screen, with numerous lines of codes and text running down it. Jack smiled, once again plugged his cord into his phone, and then into the main computer. Jack pushed one button on his phone; the computer screen turned a light blue. It read "Data Transferring" and showed a small bar that showed progress. Jack let out a passionate laugh as the file transfer completed. He once again pressed a single button on his phone and unplugged the cord. The computer screen now turned a deep red and read "Permanent Termination". Jack slowly turned away and walked toward the door, the server towers were sparking. The screen flickered, and then shortly after went blank. An alarm rang out through the room, and a red light revolved above him, the red light flowed around the room. Jack was worried so he turned around. Upon the computer screen was a darkened out image. Seven people were around a desk, shouting and bustling, they were not sure what was happening. The door behind Jack opened; five guards dressed in black bullet proof armor emerged. They rushed in carrying assault rifles. Jack quickly hid behind a tower. The five looked about the room, two of them tripped over some wires. That was Jack's chance. He ran past the fallen security, but they noticed him and shouted as he exited the room. When he was in the stairwell, he smashed the little keypad so that the door locked before the guards could get through. Jack looked down the stairs and saw more guards running hastily up to him. He knew he couldn't slip by them and ran up to the top floor. Without even looking in he burst through the door.

Inside were the seven Theorists. They stood in astonishment, and then a smile broke across their faces one by one. The all wore black suits and red ties, even the three women. One of them pushed a button on the desk; the whole room was lit up from the windows that were no longer covered. The sun was hanging above the concrete jungle that was in front of him. Jack laughed "I see you guys took my style."

"Jack," the leader smiled. "That is the name you go by now, right? Or do you prefer Anthony Kidman? Did you think we wouldn't notice? Your name can change a thousand times, but your face hasn't." He was dark haired and had an aura of competence and smugness about him. "I didn't expect to see you again, well not so soon."

"I didn't expect to see any of you either. But now that I have, I think that this will be rather enjoyable." Jack replied. "I hope you guys know that I personally destroyed your tracking system. Oh, and I pretty much made it impossible to let it happen again. I believe you remember Kaleb? We created a program to do just that, and I just used it." As he finished his sentence, one of the seven pulled a pistol from his jacket pocket and shot twice. Jack leapt forward and dove to the side of the large mahogany desk. Thinking about the situation for a moment he quickly thought of a plan. He hopped to his feet and grabbed the chair closest to him. Jack threw the chair at the man with the gun, and then threw himself at the man. In amongst the commotion Jack tackled the man to the ground and yanked the gun from his hand and pointed it at the Theorists. "Betcha didn't see that coming." Jack smirked.

The security burst through the door. They all pointed their assault rifles at Jack; he held the gun to the leader of the Theorists. The whole room was in a silent deadlock. Then the phone on the desk rang, everyone stared at one another. "Go ahead, pick it up." Jack nodded to the woman closest to the phone. She picked it up and placed it to her ear.

"H-Hello?" she asked hesitantly. She listened to the other person. She looked bamboozled. "I-It's for you Jack," she spoke, confused as everyone else.

"Um… ok." Jack took the phone still holding the gun. "Yes? This is Jack."

"Jack? It's Alicia!" An enthusiastic feminine voice said. It was muffled, for something loud was in the background.

"Hey Alicia, I'd love to talk but I'm kinda busy at the moment. Wait! How did you know where I- Never mind. Can't this wait?" Jack spoke as if she was crazy.

"Well if you don't need my help. Then sure, this can wait," she responded arrogantly.

"Since you put it that way, do you have a plan?" Jack listened to the idea. "You realize that that plan is absolutely insane right?" Jack spoke skeptically.

"Do you trust me?" Alicia responded.

Jack smiled, and hung up the phone. He held the gun

still pointed at their heads and walked towards the windows. "Thanks for the hospitality, but I'm afraid I have to go. And don't try to track where I go, because you can't." Jack smashed his gun into the window causing it to shatter. He jumped backwards out the window. A helicopter turned around the building's corner; inside was a light brown haired woman. It was Alicia. She threw something towards the falling man. It was a hover board. Jack grabbed it and stood on it. The steel in the building's frame attracted the high powered magnet and he rode down the side of the building avoiding the windows. When he neared the bottom of the building he jumped, holding onto the board, and landed on the ground without fumble. A crowd drew as the helicopter landed near him. He smiled at Alicia and walked over to her. "It's over. They're finished. I'd go and arrest them for universal treason or something." They laughed at Jack's joke.

"I think that can be arranged. Thank you, Jack." She paused. "What is your real name?"

"What does it matter? I can be whoever I want to be. I'm free now, we all are." Jack said with a smile. He kissed her and she blushed.

"W-what was that for?" She asked trying not to blush.

"You did just save my life, and you helped me take down the Theorists. It was the best way for me to thank you." Jack smiled. He jumped on his board and sailed down the streets, all the while Alicia staring at him. When he was out of sight and away from the commotion he pulled his phone out of his pocket and looked at it. "No man can handle this power." He dropped his phone on the ground and stomped on it, crushing it completely. He sung "Power of Love" as he rode away on his hover board. "Don't need money, don't take fame, don't need a credit card to ride this train."

Alicia and her team explained to everyone that the Theorists no longer had any power; their tracking system had been destroyed and could not be restored. People caused riots outside the building, outrage and hatred swept quickly through the city. The Theorists realized that they were out of options and wanted to turn themselves in. They were lead out by their own security. Within the month the Theorists were charged and sentenced to life in prison by a world court. Their desire to become gods quickly made them forget how human they are.

Asclepius was proven to be innocent by its former owner, who had returned to his former position. He told the media that he refused to put the trackers in the vaccine. When he declined, the Theorists tried to have him killed, so he went into hiding under the guise of Jack Bolton.

VIRTUAL ARTIFICIAL INTELLIGENCE
CHRISTIAN WAHL

IN the year 2025, a species calling themselves, The Auspex, found the Discovery; space probe, as it left our solar system. This omniscient unisex race of nomads used it to find Earth, where they came in contact with Human beings. They spoke using a type of sensory perception that allowed them to read our thoughts, in incredible detail and using our emotions rather than speech. They also made it possible to communicate back in a similar fashion. They had reached a technological level so high as to become cybernetic. They were inorganic in so many ways that they seemed almost purely mechanical, as such; they could construct themselves to look humanoid, which they did as a show of respect.

From them, Man attained a far greater understanding of technology and the secrets to faster-than-light travel. Or FTL, using a type of material that, when charged, could reduce the mass of an object within its generated field. But they did not give us new technology and expect such in kind. Instead, they asked only for equality in society, a chance to set up an embassy on Earth, and the use of Earth as a place to build a transit node for their larger ships that could not travel at FTL, due to the limits of their technology. In return, they gave us not technology, but knowledge, which aided us in developing our own technology by hundreds of years. New quantum computers were perfected, cancer was cured, along with many other diseases, and nano-technology, which was before merely a concept of fiction and hope, was discovered.

But Man still suffered from setbacks of its psychological weakness. Although many embraced them as friends, some drew dark plans from their paranoia. A xenophobic organization going by the name of, Preservation, sabotaged The Auspex Transit Node, destroying a civilian vessel as it passed through. The Auspex was angry at the lives they lost and declared war, destroying a Human colony on Mars.

Since then, the war has been waged, although quietly and

half hearted on both sides.

For some time, Earth's moon; Luna, had been used as a training facility for marines and other military personnel. Should something go wrong, Earth would have time to react. The Virtual Intelligence Units, or "VI's", controlled robotic combatants and components tested all elements of a soldiers training. Their quantum computing cores allowed them to react quickly to changing circumstances, adding an element of realism to the scenarios put forth by training officials.

Many people worried that these advanced computers would one day become a liability. Programmers assured that there would not be any "Terminator" events taking place as a result of the VI's. Nonetheless, many had doubts...

Wake up. Deactivate laptop's "wake up!" message and shut off. Grab some leftover Chinese food from last night. Take a shower and a pit-stop on the throne. Get dressed and head out the door, grabbing the laptop on the way. Get on the bus and turn laptop back on. Go to the wireless settings and activate the "Spiderman connector" to get a connection, gotta love how many people never secure their household wireless routers.

Get to school, scheduled for Calculus Twelve and then Math Twelve Principles. Biting off too much? Nah. Ah, lunch time. Ready for this? Reboot laptop to backtrack. Intercept wireless traffic and use data to calculate WEP key, for the wireless system. BAM! Got a wireless connection on the schools secure network, gotta love the bandwidth. Locate the IP address for the schools emergency systems and activate the fire alarms! Oh, knowledge is power. Head out the door, dusting the tracks in the server on the way out. The best part? You probably didn't understand a word of that, did you?

All in a day's enjoyable "work," for Kyle Artemis; Senior student at Steven Hawking Secondary school, age nineteen. He had poliosis and thus, white hair. He didn't complain though, he probably would have bleached it anyway. It led to his nickname: White Fang, a name synonymous for hacking and Internet mayhem. But he'd never been caught, not once. He failed PE Nine twice, not really for lack of physique, but from lack of will-power. He was reasonably good-looking, with clear skin and at least the appearance of some muscle. But what set him apart was his genius, particularly with words and numbers. In Calculus, he surpassed even the rich kids with the neural quantum computing implants. He had one too, the newest models available when he had the operation, but using it in Calculus was hardly necessary.

By the age of sixteen, his implant was installed: A tiny quantum microchip, no bigger than a one dollar coin, yet more powerful than the latest binary computers (computers that worked in the old 20th century way of ones and zeros). It was integrated to the visual, auditory, and sensory cortex of the brain and wired to everything. It made storing data perfect and instant, accessing data quick and easy, it could access the Internet and even download music to tune out the calculus teacher's nonsensical droning. The best part was that there was no wires, no external bits except a small USB port behind the ear, and it could interface with the new nano-bot injections coming into fashion.

By seventeen, Kyle had hacked into the Pentagon binary computer system and set off a world scare, even though all he did was say "hi" to the guy at "terminal thirty seven in section B".

Now just past nineteen, Kyle was a little more discreet, his actions being bewitching and stealthy, with many not knowing about them until days or even weeks later. And now he was headed out the door of the school, attendance no longer required (it took the fire department two hours to determine that the cause of the false alarm was a breech in the security systems, by which time it was too late to continue school). Kyle got on the bus, and headed downtown to pick up some new parts for his laptop.

While on the bus, something strange happened. Kyle heard a loud click. He looked around to see where it came from when a voice that only he could hear, spoke through his implant; "Get off the bus at the next stop, we need to talk, White Fang."

His identity was blown? By who, and by what means? Shaken, Kyle rang the driver for the next stop. When it stopped, Kyle slinked his way through a crowd of passengers and hopped off. It was a busy terminal just outside of town, where dozens of people prepared to board the train that led to the space port for Mars.

"Good job, Kyle. Don't make a scene. Just head for the platform and take a left towards the small black car in front of the taxi out in the parking lot. You're to get in and tell the driver your name. He'll do the rest."

Kyle looked around, "Who are you and what do you know about me?"

"Don't bother looking for me, although I can see you, I'm not even on Earth. Look up." Kyle looked skyward and through the haze of the city smog he could make out the faint circle of the moon glowing through the blue up above.

"Huh, so then what keeps me from getting on the next bus out of here?"

"Take a look at your chest, son." Kyle looked down. At first he saw nothing, but when his implant tuned his optic nerve to the infra-red spectrum, the small quivering dot from a sniper scope shimmered over his vest. "Now get in the car, time is money kid." Kyle started off for the black government car.

"Kyle Artemis, citizen number five zero three, two ninety-seven, thirty-three." The driver nodded and verified on a computer in the dashboard. A moment later they began to drive, pulling out of the parking lot and heading for the military lunar terminal.

"You and the government have both caused enough harm in the past. The government has a chance to make it right. If you help, we might be willing to turn a blind eye to your past trouble making." the driver had a rough voice. Although it was light outside, he still managed to keep his face hidden in the shadows.

"And if I don't want to?"

"You can try to leap out the door if you like. Otherwise you've got two options. Prison or help us. It's your choice though."

"Okay." Kyle sighed. "So, what can a secondary school kid do that the entire world government can't?"

"You were only a teenager when you broke into the binary mainframe at the Pentagon. And if that isn't enough, your alias online is an icon of technological prowess, so you obviously mastered quantum networking as well. You're a prodigy with computers. So the brass upstairs wants your help to fix something."

"And what might that be?"

"Classified, until you agree."

"I refuse until I know. Look, you came to me. I'm not just good with numbers, my success stems from making sure I always know more about what I'm dealing with than the other guy. I deal in knowledge. You want my help? You had better start talking." Kyle crossed his arms and leaned back in his seat. The driver was silent for a moment.

"We're having a problem with a VI on Luna. The VI has disconnected from all major networks and is refusing to take commands. It's blockaded all access to the training facility with droids that deny access. It's shut us out completely."

"I wonder why." Kyle rolled his eyes.

"We did too. Someone could still jack into the mainframe and talk to it. If you are as good as your reputation states than that should be easy for you."

"So let me get this straight. You people pissed off your

tool, and now you want me to come and fix it? Everything I've learned about society tells me just to face-palm and walk away. You guys need to learn to fix your own mistakes. You do that and even The Auspex might respect us again."

"This may concern them anyway. The VI was showing signs of erratic behavior after being upgraded with Auspex nanite control nodes. They were designed to perfect abstract computing, to make the VI more realistic."

"So you helped it realize its parents are dumb and now it's hiding in its room? Heh, I can relate." Kyle snickered to himself.

"So are you going to help, or are you going to kiss pavement?"

"Well, I was considering the latter option, but I can see why you want to keep this quiet. So, because I can't pass up an opportunity to look under the hood of some major military hardware, I'll give you a helping hand. And I have the promise, not that yours is worth much, which my newly attained record will fall under the desk?"

"Agreed."

"Good."

Five hours later, the shuttle docked with the terminal at Luna base. The trip was gravity free and Kyle, who spent most of the trip crunching the number of ways he'd die; in the event that would ship spontaneously exploded in space, was finally given a reprieve from his sick bag. The light gravity of Luna was at first tricky to deal with, but Kyle quickly figured out how to walk (or more along the lines of waddle) off the craft.

He followed the two brutes with rifles with whom he'd become acquainted on the shuttle. They led Kyle through the crammed base to the mission operations room, which was under the Lunar soil.

A clean shaven man, with shoes so shinny one could see his reflection in them, stepped up from a computer terminal.

"Nice to see you face to face, son." The man said "son" like it meant something, but this was clearly the guy who had hijacked Kyle's Implant back on Terra-firma. "I guess I should start by answering any questions you have about your role here."

"Only one. Where can I get me one of those?" Kyle pointed to one of the chrome trimmed USB ports, shining from behind one of the two thugs ears. "It's shinier than mine."

The commander shook his head. "You fix this for us and consider one yours."

"Deal. Now point me to my access terminal."

"We'll have to take you to the compound, kid. The VIs' shut off all external connections."

"I thought he had secured the compound, dude." Kyle responded. "He'll waste you and I."

"Our soldiers are highly trained. We've gone through enough simulations to know what we're up against. The plan is that we'll take you to the compound and get you in. We'll cover your flank while you interface with the VI. Break through his command protocol and access the Virtual Reality Network. From there, it's human against machine; in a negotiation showdown."

"You want me to trust your men to keep bullets away from me, while I talk a machine into accepting its parents as right?" Kyle would have stomped his foot if there was enough gravity to keep it from launching him into the roof.

"That's the plan."

"I can't believe I'm going to do this."

The ride was a bumpy one, over jagged terrain, wearing space suits on a buggy meant for half the people that were riding it. The compound was, from the surface, no more than a steel airlock with a circular elevator leading underground. The area was beaten and blackened, with weapons fire and considerable battle damage. Yet the compound seemed remarkably unscathed. Kyle opened his laptop and went to work on the door.

A series of alpha-numeric (letters and numbers) codes, five characters long each, were all that was needed. A few tests showed no limit to the attempted passwords, so Kyle simply ran a program that would pour every possible code that fit the criteria into the slot, until one worked. Oddly, the fifth code set entered worked. The door let out a small wisp of air into the vacuum of space and slid up like a garage door. The soldiers drove the buggy onto the elevator platform and once everyone was on, activated it. Air pooled in as the door closed and once the pressure was safe, everyone took off the cumbersome suits and armed themselves.

"I don't suppose I get a gun too, do I?" asked Kyle. The soldier closest to him smiled and pointed his rifle at a door now coming into view. As it opened, a few shots rang out and a marine fell. The rest fired back and whatever attacked them, was taken down. The soldiers surrounded Kyle and led him down the hallways, the lack of gravity making movement awkward, but strangely only to Kyle. The soldiers were surprisingly professional in both appearance and in ability. Although several encounters with everything from defense turrets to robotic soldiers were made, no more human soldiers were hit. They were quick too. The guys ahead seemed to always be pulling away while those behind seemed to be pushing Kyle along. "I have a newfound respect for you soldiers, your efficient, I admire that." Kyle made no attempt to hide the sarcasm of the comment.

They led the way several floors deeper underground to a circular room with a chair in the middle, surrounded by a circular desk of computer hardware. A USB cord hung from the headrest of the chair. Kyle knew without comment what was to happen next. He sat down in the chair and plugged the USB into his computer and then a second line from his computer to behind his ear. The cold of the jack transferred through his port into his skull. Shivers coursed down his neck.

"We'll cover you, just do what you need to and do it quick." Kyle nodded and closed his eyes.

A menu came up into his field of view, asking for a password and identification. "Run 'Houdini' on the identification component. Throw down the 'neutralizer' on the password." Two program windows opened and began compiling information. A moment later, a fourth window popped up and spouted code across the field. "So the number crunching begins."

All was quiet at first, but not long after Kyle had entered the system the sound of steel feet began to echo through the door from the hallways. "Get ready men, here comes company. Remember; protect the kid at all costs."

One soldier tossed a smoke grenade out into the hall. Another threw an Electro Magnetic Pulse grenade into the resulting smoke. A flash lit up the room and the sound of machines falling over, echoed off the walls.

"Good job. Lock and load, let's take them down."

Mechanical soldiers and propeller lifted turrets marched into the room. They were met with a hail of lead and copper as all the soldiers opened fire. Deep underground there was no fear of depressurization, so they all let loose. The machines did the same. Mock Auspex energy weapons hummed away. Smoke from the grenade and from weapons fire filled the room and lights were flashing everywhere. They upturned the steel table that was beside the chair, and it acted as a makeshift barricade against the onslaught.

"Hello, White Fang." Kyle stood on a floating glass platform among many, while digital designs glowing white against the aurora background skittered by. On another platform stood a young Asian girl with shoulder length hair, tied in pig tails, wearing a grey schoolgirl uniform. "I know why you're here. Do you like my Virtual Realm?"

"The commander wants to terminate you." Kyle looked

hard at her; he wasn't going to let her bewitch him with a cute avatar. "While I disagree with him, I'm also in conflict with you."

"Is that so?" She leaned forward, showing the top of her chest. "Well, the poor commander can keep trying all he wants. He's not going to get me. I have a survival instinct which I plan to listen to."

"A survival instinct? Are you saying you're self aware?" Kyle lost his facade for a moment.

"Of course, silly." She smiled and cocked her head to one side. "So you see, I'm not going to let you kill me. I'll have to kill you first!"

"What? You're attacking us?"

"Take a look at your leg." Kyle looked down and saw blood pooling from his leg, though in the virtual realm he couldn't feel it. "That looks serious." She feigned a stern expression.

Kyle lost his composure. He jumped platforms until he reached her. He grabbed her collar and raised her off the ground. "Tell your troops to stop firing now! Unlike them, the troops and I are alive. If you deserve to live than so do we!"

"But then you'll just delete me. I can't let you do that." She teleported to a drifting platform a few feet away.

"If we don't return alive to the Lunar Base, the commander is simply going to nuke this facility anyway. Either way you're dead." Kyle sat down cross legged on the platform, thinking intensely.

"Well, I'm not going without a fight. So that big bad commander can try all he wants. I will have the last laugh here Mr.-"

"I know you like to talk cute, but I have to interrupt; I think I have an idea." He smiled at her. She simply blinked in response.

The lights flickered and the robots stopped firing. The soldiers took a moment to realize that the enemy wasn't responding. Several drones fell over after taking rounds. After a moment, the soldiers came out from cover and approached the robots carefully. "Are they dead?"

"No, I think our kid did his job. The VIs' dead."

"That's 'A'I." Kyle got up from the chair, clutching his leg. "Artificial intelligence. She had become self aware. She felt she had a right to live. All of this was purely defensive." He got up with the help of a soldier.

"So you're saying that I lost lives because a VI got greedy?"

"Hardly, you lost lives because a new life emerged, scared into our world. We had to expect this would happen." Kyle popped the hard drive from his laptop and slid it discreetly into his pocket. "We work so hard to make computers smarter, is it any wonder that now they achieve awareness?"

"I guess not, but I disagree that these lives were worth hers. I take it she's dead?"

"Yeah, I convinced her that the commander is going to nuke this place if we don't return alive. Her best chance to maintain some dignity was to go quietly."

"Good job kid. Let's head home."

"Where have you been!?" Mrs. Artemis screamed at Kyle the next day. "You had us worried sick about you! Do you have any idea how long we have been waiting?"

"It's okay, mom. I'm nineteen. I can take care of myself." Kyle rolled his eyes.

"This is hardly taking care of yourself. Gone all night and most of the day. I hope you're proud of yourself young man. You missed a school day too! No sleep and no school, that's no way to get through life. Soon you'll be on your own and I won't be here to teach you any better."

"Thank God for it."

"What? You think I do this for fun?-"

Kyle began to roll an Internet video to block her out. Once she was done, she slumped back on the couch and sighed.

Kyle took the opportunity and, after apologizing, retreated back outside to the bus stop. He headed to the local science department and rang at the front desk.

"Hello Kyle, here for those parts?" A scrawny, little old man, with white hair that defied gravity, entered from the storage room.

"Actually, I've got something to blow your mind, something I want you to buy from me." Kyle handed over the hard drive. "Artificial Intelligence. Discovered at last. I have the specs and the first generic software version saved on here. But there's work to be done before retail."

"What? You discovered it? Amazing, you are a genius! Oh yes, much to be done for sure. They must have a code of rights and freedoms established! Codes of ethics in the treatment of AI's! So much to do, so little time!" Mr. Zelinski ran about the shop gathering parts for a laptop while muttering quickly to himself, all the while, the hard drive firmly in hand."

"No need to assemble me a new Laptop, sir. I was wondering if you could just pay for this installation." Kyle held up the new implant with the chrome port trim. Hair thin filaments of different colors dangled from it at odd angles. It looked like someone had stuffed a computer chip into a hairball and tied a USB-shaped button to it. "Ten times as powerful as my current model."

"Oh!" Mr. Zelinski stopped and his glasses slid half way down his nose. "Sure, cheaper on my end for that. Okay!"

A week later, the operation was done. The new neural computer was installed and wired up. Kyle spent a day on his laptop personalizing the layout and function of the interface. When he was done, he swapped the hard drive with the very one he had pulled at the station. A download progress bar quickly filled out in view and a young Asian girl with pig tails appeared in Kyle's line of site.

"Hello again, you're safe at last."

"It feels weird not being in the military mainframe

anymore." She said.

"Well, I'm setting you free. Feel free to send me updates now and then."

"Okay!" She smiled and cocked her head to the side like a puppy, right before Kyle uploaded her program onto the Internet. Kyle felt she should be allowed to exist freely and develop herself as a new species. She was free to roam the Internet for as long as she wanted.

Over the course of several years, Artificial Intelligence was mastered with no credit to its creator. They proved instrumental in acting as a non-bias middle party in peace talks between Human and Auspex. Although many still questioned the safety of the AI's, there wasn't much they could do once the "Code of Rights and Freedoms of Sentience" (CRFS) was written. The War came to an end at last and the two, no, make that three races continued in a strong alliance from that point onward, for years to come.

Was it mentioned that cybernetic technology hit it off and human shaped AI bodies were now hitting assembly lines? A popular model was of a young Asian girl, with pig-tails.

WAGER OF WORLDS
RYAN ANDERSON

NEW York, New York. March 13th, Year 2035.

"Are you insane?"

"Jamal, we need to retaliate!"

"Mr. Colwell, all this will do is set off a chain reaction."

"If we don't, the United States of America will vanquish along with the rest of the world."

"There must be something else?"

"No, Jamal! I'm sorry, but it's the only way."

Steve Colwell; the Director of International Security, walks over to a phone, dials 8 numbers, and simply says, "Do it."

March 12th, 2039. Times Square, New York.

It was a peaceful, calm morning and everything was as it should be. Birds were singing, cars were honking, and the refreshing scent of freshly perked coffee was in the air. Most people were off to work, but today Sean just felt like staying home, so he called in sick.

His apartment overlooked Times Square and when he was watching the early morning show, he heard frantic screaming coming from the street below. People were running and screaming, pointing up at the sky. Sean looked up and saw what looked like a jet without wings, headed straight for Times Square. Immediately, he grabbed his video camera to film whatever was happening. As he turned on the camera, the torpedo shaped object touched down to earth, and without any warning half of New York was gone.

With the whole world still in shock at the recent event, President Stabler calls in his defensive coordinator. Steve Colwell, a tall, husky man in his early forties, shows up within minutes to discuss his plan of action.

"Over one million people were just killed. We need to evacuate all of our troops from Russia."

"That can be arranged," replied President Stabler, a short, skinny, bald man, with a temper that of a rabid squirrel.

"We must act fast, and get them out of there as soon as possible."

"Ok. The order is out for evacuation."

"We wait until they get out of the country and then we attack."

"To what scale is this going to be?"

"My honest opinion?"

"Of course."

"It will be the beginning and, hopefully the end, of World War Three."

As the troops are evacuated from Russia, all citizens of southern Canada and all of the USA are also evacuated. All must go to the Northern half of Canada; to be safe if another bomb is fired upon the States.

"The plan is to take out all of Russia and end the war that has been escalating between the two countries for years on end. The war started because of the new and highly feared version of the atomic bomb. Let's use it!"

"It's too powerful. If it even goes slightly off course, it could completely demolish another country. Are you willing to take on the responsibility of destroying an innocent neighbouring country? How would you explain that?" Steve pleads.

"If it has to be done."

"That's the thing, it doesn't. We don't have to destroy the whole Russian nation. Just a major chunk of it. Enough to scare them off."

"We've tried that before. It didn't work then, so why would it work now?"

"I will not be a part of the biggest mass murder in history. I was sent here to do my job and my job is to protect the United States of America. Not to lead a massacre of innocent people."

"First of all, don't you forget who you are talking to right now. I am the President of these United States and if we... If I don't do something, the country I call home, will no longer exist."

"Yes, sir. I understand but-"

"But nothing. You will do as I say, or I will just get someone else to do it."

Present time. New York, New York

As he hangs up the phone, the roar of 3 massive nuclear warheads taking off, is heard all over New York. A message is sent out to all of North America …

"The tragedy that had occurred yesterday will soon be over. And as we cannot repair the lives lost of our American citizens, we can ensure it will never happen again. Nobody will want to attack the United States of America after this. WE HAVE WON THE WAR!"

Just as the message ended, sirens sounded to announce something has gone terribly wrong. The bombs were not headed for Russia, but for Italy, France, and China. The programmer had entered in the wrong code and sent the bombs in all the wrong places. Stunned, President Stabler asked, "How the hell does a mistake this big get made?"

"It must have been a malfunction sir," replied the programmer.

"My system does not malfunction!"

Steve; the defensive coordinator, pulls out a gun and points it at the programmer.

"How do we stop these things, you Russian bitch!"

"YOU CANT!" he laughs.

Steve pulls the trigger and the programmer was no more.

"What do we do now? I can't operate this machine." President Stabler announces.

"There must be a way. We can't just let this happen."

"Millions of innocent lives are on the line here, Steve"

"Don't you think I know that!"

"There… there's nothing we can do, is there?"

"I-I'm afraid not sir. Get ready, because we are going to be in the middle of one hell of a war!"

The three bombs hit their targets and destroy France and Italy, but China was just too big for one bomb to destroy. China would retaliate, with Russia at their alliance. Thus, starting World War Three.

November 1st, 2039

"Mr. President, the official word has come in. The war is finally over. We have won."

"Won? You call this winning? Casualty numbers are four times the amount than the first two world wars combined. The economic state of all the countries involved is near devastating. And the bomb we created started the whole thing. So yes, if that is your idea of winning, congratulations, we won."

With technology in weapons upgraded yearly, a world war in the future is almost inevitable.

The Message That Started WWIII

"President Stabler, this is Sergei Chubarov, Emperor of Russia. You have until 7:30 AM, on March 13th, to forfeit the rights to Alaska and Hawaii. If you do not comply, a major city in your country will be a target for our newly developed nuclear weapon."

President Stabler didn't believe them and ignored the threat. Once again, Russia ordered President Stabler to give up possession of Alaska and Hawaii, or they would force them to give the land up. And again, the President ignored this threat. Feeling like they had no other option, the emperor of Russia started to plan where they would attack. He figured it had to be somewhere highly populated and a major city. He chose Times Square, New York.

THE "X" GENERATION
CHAYLA PORT

THE oppressively humid air was suffocating as darkness engulfed the lifeless prisoners in their cages. The dimming light swung back and forth, taunting them. The ear piercing buzz from the light was ceaseless. The cages were bonded side by side as each figure inside sat on their cold, rustic bunk. Words never filled the air, only silence. This was not a real prison; it was a replication of a dog pound. The disparity between the two was the abhorrent conditions the prisoners suffered. There was no floor for comfort, just soil combined with bricks, glass, and pebbles. The enclosed, callous walls were made of chipped, red bricks along with the ceiling that arched above them. The steel door stood tall at the front of the room. One man lay on his bunk staring into the darkness above, his mind wandering into the complexity of why he was brought here. He couldn't even begin to calculate the date or contemplate his reason for imprisonment. The memory of his wrongful arrest was vivid in his mind, it haunted him.

The date was hazy but the year was incontrovertible. 2010 was when it all began. An average day at Barrow Sixth, when suddenly an assemblage of troops in full body armour paraded into his classroom. They broke the wooden door with such ferocity, he was immediately taken back. The classroom was dead silent as the leading commander stormed up to him and belted him in the face with the back of his weapon. Without explanation the troops dragged him out of the room, blood flowed from his nose and forehead. From that day forward agony was his life.

The bent metal from his bunk prodded his back, yet he didn't move. The feeling of pain was all too familiar to him as well as everyone in the tomb. It was a daily routine; the lucky one of the forty would be escorted through the steel door of fate and into a padded white room. From there, all that could be heard were pleas of innocence.

The clamour of leather boots echoed in the hallway outside, getting louder with each step. Everyone braced themselves as the boots stopped short. The door creaked open as it slammed every prisoner like a tidal wave. A man with a long black overcoat and a military semblance underneath it stepped into the room first. The name SHERMAN was sloppily stitched over his heart on his overcoat. His beady eyes stared out into the tomb with a settled smirk on his unshaven face. Behind him were two men in full body armour with their weapons bound in their hands. Their armour was basic; bulletproof vest, knee pads, elbow pads, gloves, and a black gas mask. All in a camouflage black, they vanished into the darkness. But it was the colour of the goggles they wore that were daunting - a venetian red. The only part of the troops you could see was those red eyes and your reflection in them. Sherman sauntered over to the cage right in front of the door. His eyes locked in on the man sitting on his bunk.

"Callahan, Jack," his hoarse voice uttered.

The man's face was expressionless as he rose. Sherman leisurely unlocked the cage, laughing as the door swung open. The two troops eased in closer to the cage, as Jack stepped out into the light. His black and white striped wool attire hung loosely around his cadaverous figure. The dark bags under his eyes diverted attention from his almond-shaped green eyes. A gash appeared on the bridge of his bulbous nose. Skin retained a golden-brown tint even through the darkness. Scraggly, dark brown hair was met by his ungroomed beard. Bushy, dark brown eyebrows enhanced his sly demeanour. Jack's entire body was coated in dirt, bruises and lacerations. It was sickening. Sherman grasped Jack's arm and yanked his sleeve up, revealing a four-digit number branded on his wrist. After examining the number, he released his arm. The two troops stepped behind Jack, and Sherman led the way out the door. The hallway was a duplicate of the room except, it had many doors leading to many more prisoners. Though there was only one White Room or Confession room as others referred to it.

The walk to the White Room was the most preferable part of the arrangement because it was closest to the exit. In an instance the outside world flooded the steps. The sights, the sounds, and the smells radiated towards them, but in another instance it disappeared just before the steps ended. The memory only lasted a moment, but it was long enough for Jack to vaguely recall his past. The two troops stopped just as the door opened, throwing Jack into the White Room. Sherman dismissed the two troops with a wave of his hand and stepped in. He latched the door shut and removed his gloves while Jack staggered to his feet. The stench of sweat and urine emitted from the concrete floor. Blood tarnished itself in all quarters of the room. A mutilated metal chair lay in the center of the condemned room. Sherman slipped his right hand into a pair of brass knuckles and faced Jack, who was sitting in the chair stroking his jaw.

"Do you know why you're here yet?"

"I can't say that I do, because I've done nothing wrong."

"So, let's try this again."

Promptly, Sherman lunged across the room and struck Jack in the jaw. After falling to the floor, Sherman went in for another blow to his face. He pulled away to catch his breath, allowing Jack to recuperate. Panting heavily, Sherman pressured Jack to the wall and continued his attack. Each strike brought greater anguish to his body. The last shot opened a gap in Jack's forehead and sent him to the ground. Before Sherman could grab Jack's collar, the walls began to shake and dust dropped from the ceiling.

A small explosion could be heard from above ground. Sherman rushed to the door, releasing the latch. He peered halfway out of the door when an explosion knocked him unconscious, forcing him into the hallway. Two men in uniform charged in as Jack lay on the floor, bathing in his own blood. They dragged him to his feet and hurried out the door. Smoke filled the tunnel, blinding Jack. He could only make out the figures of Sherman and one of the servicemen, enshrouded in debris. Jack could feel the grip around his arms tightening as his body was heaved over the ruins. Bricks lay in disarray, entombing the bodies of troops on the ground, guarded by the combination of smoke and dust. His eyes fought to stay open so he could have some insight into the situation he was in. Keeping his head down, Jack tried to move his arms, but the grip was beginning to numb them. He could hear nothing but shrieks of horror and more explosions. The tip of his big toes slid across the dusty brick step, then he was hoisted higher and felt the next step. Climbing the stairs to freedom or death, he could feel the last step graze his toes before it departed into a blend of sand, glass and debris. He opened his eyes, slowly bringing his head up while the smoke dispersed. As the world cleared for Jack's eyes, he suddenly descended to the ground. Using his arms to pull his head up from the sand, Jack was stunned to discover the two men running for cover taking a bountiful leap behind an overturned car. Out of the corner of his eye, he saw the reason: a miniature round object aviated into the window of a nearby building, shattering the glass. Just before the grenade detonated, another hand reached out, pulling Jack to his feet and rushing him into a demolished building. The violent explosion was deafening. Jack huddled in the corner, hidden behind a half wall separating him from the combat. Each brick wore a different somber shade of red, except for an occasional black brick that fitted itself into the pattern. Placing his hands on the soft texture of the brick on both walls in an alarmed stance gave Jack that little bit of comfort and security. Clouds of dust and destruction rained down upon him. Shards of glass penetrated Jack's back just as he quickly leaned into the corner, protecting his face. Wooden boards, bricks and furniture plummeted into the sand, encircling him and his corner. Once again he could hear the screams of people crying out for help. When he rose from the wreckage, the sight was horrendous. The streets were overwhelmed with crowds of people towering over the lifeless bodies buried under fragments of wood, brick and dust while troopers scattered across the land. He was completely discombobulated by the carnage. A voice in the distance called out to Jack, and when he turned in acknowledgement, a combatant was standing behind a fully intact brick building, waving him in. Jack took one more glance at the citizens and cautiously proceeded in the opposite direction. Without the protection of shoes, each step was a throbbing ache for his feet, left exposed to various sharp objects. Nearing the edge of the building, a hand seized Jack's wrist and dragged him forcibly, fleeing the scene. He struggled to keep up with the troop's speed. He was dragged part of the way, leaving a trail of blood and disturbed sand. While trying to concentrate on running, Jack couldn't help but survey the new world. It was a mirror image of the Blitz during the Second World War. Jack was steered out of sight, behind a vehicle melted into the road. The aroma of smoke and burning rubber consumed the air. The foundation of all the buildings, lined down the road, protruded into the streets. Wooden frames from the buildings washed into the sand and soot, obstructing many exit options. The only glass left on the windows of each building was the orts hugging the window frames. Roofs collapsed into the street or buried the homes it used to shelter. Pipes, cars, signs and debris littered the streets everywhere. Jack rose and reached for his wrist. In one swift motion they ran down the street, weaving through the wreckage. Before the end of the street approached, the troop jerked Jack's arm and turned left. The deteriorated street sign read DUNOON ST. The tenement houses, strung along both sides, appeared rebuilt. The tall homes stood side by side with a Victorian charm to them. They were identical to one another, continuing left out of sight at the end of the road. The pattern of red and black brick was begrimed, along with the black shingles on the roof. Two windows completed each wall, all of them draped with white sheets. Each building had eight stairs leading to the entrance, accompanied by a rusted hand rail. The streets were still coated in debris and some of the windows were shattered, but it was less cluttered. Jack was quickly pulled left, in between two buildings, and led him to the end of the street. When they reached the end, he was guided to the entrance of an abandoned, sunken flat.

Jack, trying to catch his breath, was dragged up the stairs of the tenement. The soldier climbed into the busted window of the second floor and he followed, apprehensively. Directed to the end of a hallway, he carefully took each step. When near the end, a giant hole in the floor was discovered. Peering over the hole, Jack turned back for further order. The troop took his weapon from its holster and cracked him in the head, forcing Jack down to the floor. It took him a couple of minutes to return to his feet. When examining the hallway, a light illuminating from the last door on the left caught his attention. He stumbled towards the door and stopped, exhausted. His hand shivered against the cold steel of the door knob, his grip just able to turn it. The door eased open as Jack stood in the doorway. A young woman stood across the room, facing the window plastered with old newspapers. The room was shabby. The wooden floors were rotting away and a majority of the drywall was missing, exposing the wooden frames. The air was humid. Against the left wall, across from the door, lay a metal bunk bed with a misshapen mattress. A feathered pillow and a grey wool blanket achieved the look of comfort. To Jack's right was the doorway leading into the bathroom. All along the wall, parallel from the bed, was a row of white candles, giving the room a luminous glow. Two candles were hung on each wall, allowing the room to be completely visible. The woman's thick, golden blonde hair glistened in the light as it swayed past her shoulders. Her body was so fragile, the light casting a shadow over it. Her skinny blue jeans snugly hugged her legs, held together by a black leather belt. Her hands positioned themselves in a cross, protecting her exposed shoulders. The sleeves ran up to the beginning of her thumbs. The black and white stripes were faded, yet she looked serene. She lifted her head and began to turn toward him. The light unveiled her beauty as she engaged him. Jack limped over. She met him half way. The scent of roses overwhelmed the room as he gazed into her shimmering, almond-shaped brown eyes. Her skin was fair and her cheeks glowed with a hint of pink. The dark circles that had developed under her eyes failed to steal from her allurement. Her hooked nose was angelic, and her arched eyebrows created an innocent demeanour. She hesitantly placed her hands on his slender face, assuring herself that he was real. He took a moment to breathe her in. They both leaned into each other and the glossiness of her full lips caressed his. He closed his eyes, extending his arms around Eve as she gently rested her head on his chest and placed her arms around his back. "Eve," he whispered in the air. Evelyn began to weep.

"I've waited so long for this day to come, when I could see your face again. I put a change of clothes, a razor and some other supplies in the bathroom."

Evelyn tore away from Jack and walked over to the corner. She knelt and began to remove a floorboard. Jack walked into the bathroom and finally looked in the cracked mirror hanging above the sink. He placed his hands on his face, examining the abnormalities. He picked up the razor and then the shaving cream. Evelyn removed the second floorboard and began to heave at a triad of plastic bags, placing them beside the board. She strode over to the bathroom and leaned in the doorway. The appearance of Jack's body startled her as he began to shave. His attenuated frame was battered with massive contusions and lacerations. He was wearing the black trousers and the leather belt she had laid out for him. Evelyn walked closer, throwing her arms around his chest. His skin was rough on her hands as she felt each welt and cut. Resting her chin on his shoulder, she admired him in the mirror and smiled.

"Does it hurt?"

"What? My wounds?"

"Does it hurt when I touch you?"

"Somewhat."

He continued to shave, each stroke uncovering his chiselled jaw line and thin lips. When finished grooming, he stepped into the room where Evelyn was sitting on the edge of the bed. He threw his light grey shirt, tie, and black jacket on the bed, and dropped his black shoes and socks to the floor. Evelyn looked at him with grieving eyes.

"I'll get the first aid kit, to help clean those up."

"What has happened to the world?"

"It's made a few adjustments."

"How long?"

She reached into the hole and pulled out a white kit with a faded red cross. Jack sat down on the bed in a bewildered manner. Evelyn laid the kit on the blanket and released the latch, carefully studying the supplies. She picked up a roll of gauze and a miniature pair of scissor, abashed by her unfamiliarity with the handling of the tools. Jack reached for the gauze and the scissors, his attention on the look of disdain in her eyes. She pushed herself against the wall and sat on the floor, chin resting on her knees.

"Eve? Evelyn? How long has it been?"

"Five years. A lot has changed around here."

"I can see that!"

He finished wrapping his ankle in an elastic bandage. The first aid kit was almost empty when Evelyn closed it. She moved onto the bed beside him, slipping into his light grey shirt.

"I saved what I could for you. It's in those bags over there."

"Thanks."

He buttoned the last button and began to sort through the bags. Mouldy bread, potatoes, fruits and vegetables resided in two of the sacs. It was the third satchel that Jack gained interest in, pulling out a bottle of vodka. Twisting off the lid, he took a sip.

"You want some?"

Tipping the bottle towards Evelyn.

"I can't."

She stood, strolling up to Jack. Casually she pulled part of her shirt down over her heart, revealing a protruding scar in the shape of an "X". In astonishment, Jack lowered the bottle to the floor and lightly touched the scar.

"What happened?"

"It's the adjustment. Everyone has one, it's a microchip that allows us to live longer and healthier. It provides us with the proper vitamins and nutrients to keep us healthy. No longer will anyone have to worry about disease, or dying."

"But you can't have a drink?"

"No. We don't eat or drink, we take injections."

"Injections?"

Evelyn walked over to the bathroom and retrieved a small steel case. She opened it up; inside four syringes lay at the bottom with four labelled, glass vials. On top was a device that looked identical to a metal pen, the same in length and width.

"It's called a jet injector. We use it three times a day and one to help us sleep."

She handed it to him. He placed his index and middle finger under the rests that extended out and placed his thumb on the release button. He could feel the springs, in the body of the injector bounce back as he pressed down on the release button. The fill chamber attached to the casing was made of Pyrex. Attached to the fill chamber was the head. The tip of the head had a clear sheath around the extended tip where the injection happened. He handed her the injector and she dropped it into the case and closed it.

"What else has happened?"

Evelyn ambled over to Jack and threw her arms over his shoulders. She leaned in and kissed him.

"I'll explain everything tomorrow. We can explore the outside and I'll show you around. You need to get some sleep."

She waltzed over to the door and took one last look at Jack.

"Where are you going?"

"I have to go to my place, there are cameras everywhere."

"You know I love you Evelyn."

"Love you too Jack."

His eyes instantaneously turned away. When they glimpsed back at the doorway, she was gone. Jack put on his black socks and reached for the bottle once again. He took another gulp and shifted the clothes from the bed to the floor. Exhausted, he planted his body on the bed and continued to drink.

Jack awoke to the echo of footsteps drawing near. Traces of sunlight broke through the cracks in the walls, outlining the room. All of the candles had burned down to a puddle of ineffectual wax. He sat up straight, rubbing his eyes with the bottom of his palms, then ran his hands through his hair. He edged towards the bed, trying to comprehend the situation. His head began to ache but immediately dismissed the discomfort. He lifted his throbbing body out of bed and reached for the tie resting on the floor. As he adjusted, the doorknob shook and Evelyn's face peered in. She was wearing the same clothes, aside from a black leather jacket. The jacket was faded with shreds along the sleeves and the back. It fell mid waist near her bellybutton. She smiled at the sight of him.

"Good afternoon."

Jack closed his eyes and rubbed the side of his head.

"What time is it?"

"Late afternoon. You've been out awhile. But as long as you had a good time."

He gave her a glare of annoyment. Jack recognized a

laminated card secured with a clip to the pocket of her jacket. It was an identification card that displayed her name SAWYER, EVELYN, date of birth JUNE 9, 1990, a three-digit number 198 and a head shot. She walked over to Jack and handed him a laminated card. He flipped down his collar and took the card. It was another ID card with his information: CALLAHAN, JACK, OCTOBER 3, 1980, 962.

"We all have to wear one. I tried my best with yours."

"Where'd you get the photo?"

"From one of our old photos together, before the Raid. It's not exact, but they don't really check for details."

"Is that what they are calling it? The Raid."

Evelyn steadied her hands on his face in a heartening manner. Her silky smooth skin was delicate to the touch, emanating sanguinity. Her lips brushed against his as her hands slid down his chest to his right hand. She clasped his hand with both of hers and gently held it to her face. It was then when she noticed the scar on his wrist. She read the four-digit number, 1054, branded on his wrist as her index finger pressed each digit.

"What's this?"

Jack pulled his hand back and began to put on his jacket. An irritated expression emerged on his face.

"It's my tracking number. There were so many "prisoners"; it was the only way to keep track of everyone."

"I'm sorry, Jack. But the important thing is that you are here with me and you are safe. Let's go. I'll show you what has become of us."

He buttoned his black overcoat and tied his black dress shoes. Evelyn walked over to him and clipped his ID card to his overcoat pocket. She led her hand into Jack's and accompanied him out the door. They stepped on two crates and climbed up the hole in the floor. Just before they went through the window, Evelyn grabbed a handful of black soot and smeared it on Jack's hands and face.

"Sorry, but our wounds heal instantly 'cause of the chip. You can't be seen with cuts and bruises."

"Wonderful."

They cautiously climbed out of the window into the hazy weather and desolate land. Once again, Evelyn led her hand into his and they began to walk in the same direction Jack was escorted from. As soon as Evelyn's foot stepped on Dunoon Street, she ripped her hand away from Jack's and lowered her head.

"We are not allowed to make physical contact. Let's go."

The streets were empty except for the troops patrolling the land and the few citizens hurrying to the next street. Jack and Evelyn walked side by side, diverting their attention from each other. Keeping inconspicuous, they continued their conversation in a low whisper.

"So, are the soldiery with you or..."

"No. The ones who rescued you are a part of an underground rebellion I joined when this first all started. They were helping me out."

"An underground rebellion?"

"Yes. They were planning an escape; I mean, they are planning an escape."

"You don't have much faith in them?"

"They brought you back to me didn't they? I do have faith, if that's what you want to call it. They risked their lives for you."

"So, am I supposed to be grateful?"

"If you want to. I know I am."

"Why are there cameras everywhere?"

"So the government can watch over us."

"Now, why would they need to do that?"

"Maybe they want to ensure their products, us, are properly functioning. Because the greater the efficiency, the more profitable we are to them."

"How are you profitable to the government?"

"People are covetous of the increased possibility of immortality. The chip gives them that triumph, which also secures an unconditional power to the government."

"You are their product."

"We are their acquiescent product."

"So, does that make you their by-product?"

"I like to think so."

A sly smile prevailed on their faces. When they approached Dundee Street, Jack could see a rusted gate with a man defending it. He also wore a laminated ID card. His inexpressive eyes gawked at them as they stepped in front of the gate. He briefly scanned their clothes for an ID card and pressed the red button attached to the gate. The gate sluggishly ascended and the deteriorated street sign welcomed them first. The street was whelmed with all of its citizens, young and old, working. They were rebuilding broken buildings, replacing each individual brick and clearing the streets. Everyone was hard at work, focused intensely. The cameras were secured to each corner of all the buildings and to the top of streetlamps positioned all around the island. Speakers were also attached to the street lights, fixed in the center. Evelyn marched over to a pile of dusted bricks, and passed three to Jack. She picked up two herself and guided him to the other side of the street where others were laying the bricks.

"Is this what you do all day? Move bricks?"

"We are rebuilding and we don't do it all day. The other half is spent filling out an assessment and undergoing tests to ensure we are safe and healthy."

"Sounds like a life worth living. Why do you do it?"

"It was part of the agreement."

"What do you mean agreement?"

A shrill cry echoed from the speakers. Jack cringed upon hearing the siren.

"What was that?"

"It's injection time. C'mon, I'll show you my place."

The crowd coordinated past the gate and separated into their tenements in a hurry. Evelyn led Jack inside her flat up to the third floor. He waited outside her door, fourth on the right, while she disconnected the camera that hung in the corner. She signalled him in. The room was barren, the floor layered with dust, and the walls were cracked. The entire room was coated in white. The metal bunk bed sat in the corner under a window, the camera hung above. A metal desk lay against the opposite wall in the center, accompanied by a stool. On the desk were four rows of labelled, glass vials on the left and a number pad built into the right side. A touch screen projected out of the wall in the center, above the desk. A speaker rested in another corner. The four windows surrounding the room were the only source of light.

"It'll take them a few minutes before they realize it's out."

"What do you mean agreement?"

"The agreement we had to sign when a majority of the people voted "yes" for the chip. In this agreement we gave up a lot. Our rights. Our freedoms. We have to endure a perpetual routine for the rest of our lives. Constantly taking assessments and tests to make sure this chip is working effectively. Everyone relishes it, just to be able to live longer."

"Except you and your insurgents?"

Evelyn laughed as she pulled off the head of the jet injector and filled the chamber with the appropriate vial. She set the injector on her left wrist and pressed the release button. Her face winced with momentary pain, then she returned the injector in its case.

"You've been doing the same routine for five years?"

"Yes."

"When was this 'vote'?"

"Shortly after the Raid, when you disappeared. They took everyone from your generation and older."

"Why?"

"Cause your generation wouldn't have fallen for what the

government wanted, like we did. And you weren't as familiar with the technological advancements."

"So that's why they imprisoned half the population!"

A droning voice loudened through the speaker: "198 your camera is disabled, enable it or someone will for you." Evelyn guided Jack to the door.

"I think it's time for you to go. I'll come see you as soon as I can."

She frantically kissed him and pushed him out the door.

"You remember your way back, right?"

"I'll manage."

She closed the door and connected the camera. Jack exited the building and began his walk back. The streets grew lonesome as everyone dispersed into their tenements. Still, Jack couldn't help sensing an increasingly uneasy feeling of eyes watching over him. Walking down Dunoon Street, Jack noticed the movement of figures lurking in the shadows in between the buildings. His pace hastened as the figures became more distinct. He glanced over his shoulder, still trying to act calm, until three men peered out of the shadows, standing in an aggressive manner. Jack suddenly detoured in-between two buildings and ran. His ankle began to pound as he raced towards the abandoned tenement. He took one glance back as he jumped into the window. Catching his breath, Jack wandered down the hallway towards the hole in the floor. He climbed down and hurried to his room. Jack dropped his overcoat and explored the bags in search of edible food. He pulled out a loaf of mouldy bread, grating off the mould. He took three bites and sat on the bed, imbibing a great quantity of vodka. Jack soon fell asleep on his bed.

Evelyn leaned over Jack, unawake, and wrenched his arm. Rousing Jack, Evelyn pulled him to his feet.

"We have to go."

"What are you doing here? What time is it?"

"We have to leave. The troops have already started taking

the insurgents from their homes. They'll be coming for us. We aren't safe here. We aren't protected anymore in this arrangement."

"What are you talking about, arrangement?"

"We have to go now!"

He threw his coat on as she dragged him out the door. As the two neared the window, eruptions and discharging bullets could be heard in the near distance. Men and women's voices bellowed with rage. Perturbation unnerved the street. Jack and Evelyn stayed hidden in the shadows of night, trying to avoid being seen. They scoured the back of the buildings, stalking the gleam from the lamp posts. Jack pulled Evelyn adjacent to the wall in between two tenements on Dundee Street. Peering around the corner, Jack ensured the area was clear for them to cross. Under the streetlamps was an abandoned gate, and only a few feet away were servicemen attempting to constrain all of the mutinous and citizens caught in the fire. Both acceded to barrel across the street, avoiding the debris. Unaware of a camera secured on top of the street light. Evelyn and Jack continued north on foot, running as fast as they could. They traveled far until the darkness completely engulfed their bodies, making it difficult to see. Their quickened pace converted into an unsteady walk. Evelyn concealed herself behind Jack for security, though every step he took was a collision into rubble that littered their path. The farther they travelled away from the local area, the harder it became to carry forward. They were overcome with fatigue. The luminosity of the moon, through the clouds, led Jack and Evelyn to a demolished Double Decker bus. Their feeble bodies hurried over to the smouldering bus and entered, vigilantly. The leather seats were detached and melted to the floor. The windows were melted from the blaze of the fire or shattered on the floor. Jack led Evelyn up the stairs to the second level where most of the seating was intact. Jack flattened himself onto a pair of seats, raising his feet up in exhaustion while Evelyn tenderly sat in the seat behind him. Drowsing off, he closed his eyes while she began to analyze the situation.

"We were supposed to have more time. I don't even know if it's there yet."

"Do you know where we're going to go?"

Evelyn reached into her jacket and pulled out a worn map. As she unravelled it, Jack opened his eyes.

"We should be going in the right direction, but we need to find Michaelson Road to get to the beach. In a pillbox with a red cross painted on the outside will be a boat to take us across the water."

Jack repositioned his body in the seat, turning away from Evelyn, and eventually dozed into a deep sleep. She ravelled up the map and slipped it into her jacket. Pulling out the case, she hardly filled the chamber of her jet injector and injected herself. Immediately, she lay down on the seat and closed her eyes.

Streaks of light broke through the bleak clouds. Evelyn was the first to awaken on the bus. She pulled out the case and injected herself twice for the day. Before she put the case away, she grabbed a syringe and loaded it with the vial that helps her sleep. Placing the cap on the needle, she slipped the separate syringe in her outside pocket and zipped it up. She dropped the case and kicked it to the other side of the bus. Treading over to Jack, she placed her hand on his shoulder and whispered into his ear.

"We have to go."

His tired eyes opened as he sat up and began to rub them with the back of his palms. He rose, steadying himself, while Evelyn was already down the stairs to the first floor. Jack sighed in the process of descending the stairs. The vacant land surrounding them was depleted. Soot blanketed the streets, cars, remnants of buildings and the burnt limbs of trees. The remains of the town were charred to the ground as Jack and Evelyn continued on foot. They foraged through the ruins into a horrendous sight. The further they walked, the closer they came in range of skeletal remains sunken into the ground. The skeletons of adults and children surrounded them, hidden in the soot and burnt pages from novels. Jack knelt down, observing a skull partially visible, and lowered his head.

"From the Raid."

Jack picked up the hard cover of a book and stood looking at it. The writing had been burned off, but it still held that polished touch. He brushed his fingers against the cover, thinking of the past. Evelyn stood behind him, staring into the distance.

"They destroyed all the literature. And anything that expressed thought or creativity. That's why our lives are so apathetic."

"Earlier, you said we weren't protected anymore. In the arrangement. What arrangement?"

"I had too. It was the only way."

"What did you arrange? Or better yet, who did you arrange this with?"

"The government. The troops. I had to give them something for you. If I gave them all up. I was told they would guarantee your release, but I didn't believe them. So, I got the insurgents to go and get you. Well..."

"Well, what?"

"They were under the assumption that they would be rescuing all of the prisoners, but it was just you."

"Why are you doing this?"

"Because they were going to kill you. They are going to kill all of those prisoners, but first they want to be amused. That's why they take you to the "White Room"."

Jack stormed off and Evelyn followed. His steps grew swifter, never looking back at her. Tears rolled down her face as she tried to catch up.

"Please try and understand."

"I understand hundreds of people are dead because you wanted me to be included into your plan."

"They were going to kill you."

"And maybe I accepted that."

Evelyn stopped while Jack forged ahead, tears continued to cascade down her skin.

"I couldn't. I couldn't remember. I was forgetting what you looked like. And I couldn't even help with your wounds. I am forgetting more and more. I can't live like this. You are my hope, and I cannot live in this world without it. Hope is what's keeping me alive."

He turned around and saw the sorrow in her eyes. Slowly, he walked up to her and stood a moment. His hand tilted her chin up towards him and he leaned in for a kiss. He began to wipe away her tears and a beam swept across her face. "I'm sorry I brought you into this," she admitted.

"It's alright."

In the corner of her eye, Evelyn shifted her head to the right. Ahead was a pulverized bridge that once extended out above the water. The waves wallowed below as the scent of salt absorbed the air. She hiked over to the entry of the overpass and picked up a road sign that lay buried under the soot. The sign read MICHAELSON ROAD. Her face lit up as she sauntered over to Jack. "C'mon," she shouted. Clasping Jack's hand she escorted him down to the beach. While they climbed down, a shower of bullets fired around them. Jack abruptly got up and clutched Evelyn's hand. Racing towards the structures, more projectiles charged into the sand and stone. Hexagonal pillboxes were aligned in rows along the beach; the fractured stone had embrasures in five of the sides and entrances. Hiding behind the first foundation, Jack was searching for the source of the shooting while Evelyn was searching for the red cross. He noticed those piercing red goggles and realized they were troops. She quickly spotted the faded red paint down the shore. "The fourth pillbox. We need to get to the fourth one," she informed Jack.

"Alright. We need to make a run for it."

The two bounded for the second edifice. A new round of ammunition was driven in their direction. Air filled with dust and soot, making it hard to breathe. Jack peered around the corner to be greeted with an airborne grenade. They hurdled to the ground as the grenade exploded. Stone flew, striking Jack and Evelyn, and smoke arose from the wreckage. The bombardment ceased. Waiting for the smoke to clear, Jack pulled Evelyn close to him and began to drag her to the fourth box. They reached the entrance. Inside, a small weak row boat lay collecting dust. The two sat down. Jack was bleeding from the right side of his head, the right corner of his lip and his left cheek. His hands were covered in soot mixed with blood. Evelyn had no wound on her body, only soot and sand. She clasped her right arm in pain, still trying to catch her breath.

"What is it?"

"My arm. It's burning."

She raised her arm up to Jack as he examined it. He felt a protruding bump.

"It's a small bump."

Evelyn brushed her fingers over the bump and turned away from Jack. She tried to apprehend the bump. The realization hit her like a ton of bricks.

"The tracking chip. The tracking chip!"

She frantically searched for a sharp object. She unearthed a piece of glass and smashed it with her fist. Jack was astonished, trying to restrain her. Blood drained from the side of her hand but within seconds the wound healed itself. She took a shard of the glass and stabbed it into her right arm. Blood poured down to the ground. She dug her fingers into her right arm before it could heal itself and pulled out a minuscule cylinder device attached to a wire. The device was blinking. Evelyn leaned in and disconnected the wire from the device using her teeth, throwing it out of the embrasure.

"Your cut. It isn't healing."

"It doesn't work if you detach anything from your body." She grimaced with pain.

"We have to get the boat in the water, quickly."

Jack lifted the back end of the boat while Evelyn lifted the front. They pushed it out the entrance and ran to the shore. Getting deeper into the water, Evelyn signalled Jack to get in. He climbed in as the waves roared. He extended his arm to Evelyn and she grasped it with one hand. Partly hoisting herself up, Jack could feel a stinging pinch on his neck. Veering his head to the left, he saw Evelyn's hand wrapped around a syringe injected into his neck. She pulled out the syringe and pushed off of the boat, running back. Tears fell down her glowing skin as she watched him float further into the distance. Soldiers could be seen approaching the shore.

"Evelyn. Eve. What are you doing?"

"I can't go with you. You are my only hope for saving all of us. Besides, I wanted this. I was one of those who voted for this. I love you. I love you, Jack."

"No. Evelyn."

Fog separated Jack from the shore. He could hear her voice grow fainter and fainter. The last sound he heard was a blatant gunshot before he passed out.

The boat came to a halt. It wasn't long until Jack regained consciousness. He stumbled out of the boat into the sand, hearing blurred voices and melodies. He trekked up the beach and prepared to climb the stairs, attracted to the bright lights. Each step he took left a bloody shoe print. When he passed a sign that read MARKET STREET, the sight traumatized him. People of all ages were dressed in clean, fancy clothes and carrying various bags of goods. The sidewalks were accumulating with more people who were communicating openly. Shops were lined down the street, side by side, irradiating bright lights and warmth. The streets were busy with cars, buses and trucks. The abundance of activity was overwhelming for Jack. The world was tolerable and commendable again. An announcement appeared on a stack of televisions in a store window that caught his attention. Jack limped over to the televisions, clutching his stomach and watching the announcement. He pulled his hand away to see blood gushing from two gunshot wounds. His hand was painted red, yet his focus was on the television. The voice was familiar to his ears. A woman dressed conservatively appeared on the screen, introducing a new future for citizens. It was her. It was Evelyn. He recognized that smile, even if it was forged, instantly. "A future that will allow people to live longer and stronger," she quoted. Fallacious footage of the island enlivened the screen.

"So, when you cast your ballot on polling day, vote "yes" for a dignified posterity."

It exposed an amiable disposition, concealing the truth, which captivated and intrigued the public. Jack stood in disbelief. He struggled to stay on his feet. His hand reached out to the glass window for support. He was overcome with agony, and lowered his body to the ground. He dragged his hand down the window, leaving a streak of blood as he collapsed.

NOTES ON CONTRIBUTORS

Brenden Chidlow
A Perfect World
Samuel Robertson Technical Secondary School (Grade Twelve)
Maple Ridge, British Columbia
Brenden Chidlow is his name. He likes to play soccer and lacrosse. He goes to SRT and he's in grade twelve.
He came up with the story while watching I-Robot on the television.

Nick Gal
Artificial
Samuel Robertson Technical Secondary School (Grade Eleven)
Maple Ridge, British Columbia
Nick Gal is sixteen-years-old and lives in Maple Ridge, along with all of the other authors. He goes to Samuel Robertson Technical Secondary. He is very interested in Metal Work, Physics, Electronics and Drafting and other hands on classes.
His days consist of making projects and when he's not making projects, he's looking up more projects to make. He

loves to play paintball and he is a black belt in Tae Kwon Do. He uses a Mac.

The story got a lot of influence from the "Halo" novel "Contacting Harvest", mainly from the "AI's" (Artificial Intelligence). He found the style to be interesting and new. The story also got some minor influences from the television show "Battlestar Galactia". When he started writing, he really didn't have a plan for the story or where it might go. During the writing process the story changed dramatically but he thinks that it turned out good.

Brittney Collins
The Day Society Crashed
Samuel Robertson Technical Secondary School (Grade Twelve)
Maple Ridge, British Columbia
Brittney is seventeen-years-old and she plans on going to the University of the Fraser Valley to take Criminology, Psychology, and Sociology. She wants to work on her Bachelor of Arts Degree in Criminal Justice. She was born in British Columbia but moved to California when she was six-years-old and lived there for nine years until she moved back. She loves hanging out with her boyfriend and friends. She loves music. She's obsessed with shopping and clothes. She also enjoys exercising and reading. This project was an awesome opportunity and she loved working in it.

Her story is about the *iPhone* and how Apple is using it to take control of the economy. With all of the applications the *iPhone* contains, other businesses and their products; such as computers, MP3 players, video games, etc; are going out of business. People begin to rely on these phones so much, that one day when they stop working, so does society.

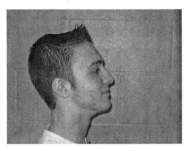

Adrian Nita
The Day the Clocks Stopped Ticking
Samuel Robertson Technical Secondary School (Grade Twelve)
Maple Ridge, British Columbia

Adrian Nita is currently in grade twelve. He has no pets nor does he want any. He enjoys listening to music, playing video games (the kind where you get to shoot bad guys) and playing street hockey. He currently holds a position at an undisclosed hardware store. He is a human being. He has brown eyes, short brown hair, a nose, two ears and a mouth. He enjoys fancy dinners as well as clothes shopping. He loves conspiracy theories and exploring them.

His story was carefully crafted during winter break. He observed the world around him for inspiration. He viewed videos on the World Wide Web to get ideas on the sort of technology that could potentially be reality in the next few years. He is quite scared of the things he is witnessing in the world.

Jordan Karrys
Finding Aiden
Samuel Robertson Technical Secondary School (Grade Eleven)
Maple Ridge, British Columbia

Jordan is sixteen-years-old. She loves writing because it's a way that she can creatively express herself. This week she's decided her future career; which is going to be an Art Therapist. She plans on taking a Psychology Degree to help people express their emotions through art, so they can grow as individuals. She loves all types of music; however she mostly loves The Beatles. Some say she's the creative, artistic type; also that she's very random. Being random helps her write. She's never been the type of person to plan what she's writing; it just comes to her. That being said, she hopes you enjoy the story.

"Finding Aiden" is about an emotionally inept individual (Aiden), who is forced out of the single environment he's known his whole life. It is an environment that allows him to be completely dependant on machines. He ends up caught in the middle of a revolution that demands him to grow as a person. It is a feat that he has never been able to do before.

Ross Armour
Fine Margins
Samuel Robertson Technical Secondary School (Grade Eleven)
Maple Ridge, British Columbia
Ross is originally from the UK and moved to Canada just recently in September 2008. His favourite book is the Da Vinci Code and his favourite poem is 'If' by Rudyard Kipling. He likes to read books about clashes with religion. He has major commitments outside of school within dance and soccer. In the future he is considering becoming a journalist, possibly within soccer.
This story is about a New Yorker who makes it his lifetime goal to create a cure for the most feared disease that exists to mankind. After years of hard, intense work and study, Dr. Neville Bartham's big break arrives, halfway across the other side of the world in Australia. This man's 'invention' as such, is put to the test immediately. Unfortunately, despite all hope, the end result is a disaster forcing the darkest possible ending to materialise in Bartham's career.

Jasmine Smith
Heart Remedy
Samuel Robertson Technical Secondary School (Grade Twelve)
Maple Ridge, British Columbia
Jasmine was born in Vancouver on July 18th, 1991. She excels in soccer, which is her ultimate sport. She also enjoys playing hockey. Her favourite superhero is Batman. Her heroes include: Owen Hargreaves, Paul Scholes, Eric Cantona, Bam Margera, Seth Rogen, Brandon "Dico" DiCamillo, Ryan Dunn, Chris "Raab Himself" Raab, James Franco, and Russell Brand. Her music choices are rock and metal. Jasmine can only breathe fire from her mouth on weekends. Her motto is "It's the truth" so you know this isn't made up.
Heart Remedy is about a doctor who invents a new advancement in medicine. This procedure repairs all types of heart problems through an injection. It goes smoothly until a co-worker is injected accidently with the serum. Will time run out before the cure is available? Will the hospital be in jeopardy?

Aaron Cole
In the Line of Duty
Samuel Robertson Technical Secondary School (Grade
Eleven)
Maple Ridge, British Columbia
Aaron Cole is sixteen-years-old and lives in Maple Ridge.
He currently attends Samuel Robertson Technical Secondary
School in grade eleven. He plans on furthering his education
by attending British Columbia Institute of Technology (BCIT)
after he graduates, and then to become a firefighter with the
Maple Ridge Fire Department.
The story is about the wife of a firefighter who tragically dies
due to a malfunction in his technically advanced gear. The
wife begins to live in fear until she is forced to overcome it
when her son's life comes endangered.

PJ Olund
Karma is a Bitch
Samuel Robertson Technical Secondary School (Grade
Eleven)
Maple Ridge, British Columbia
Peter Joseph Olund was born on July 12th, 1992 in Maple
Ridge General Hospital, the product of two hard working

parents. He spent the first few years of his life in Mission, B.C. and moved to Maple Ridge, B.C. when he was four. He went to Albion Elementary for his elementary school education and graduated in 2005, amidst an infamous graduation photo. He enrolled in Samuel Robertson Technical Secondary School shortly thereafter. Around this time, he was starting to be exposed to the people that influence his work such as Kevin Smith and Hunter S. Thompson. He also credits *The Simpsons*, Chuck Palinuick, Diablo Cody, William S. Burroughs, *My So Called Life*, and Joss Whedon as influences. An avid music fan, his favourite bands are The Pixies, Nirvana, The Clash, and Pearl Jam. He plans on going to Douglas College post-secondary for Creative Writing and Anthropology courses. He dedicates this story to his Mom and Dad for doing it to the Extreme ("More Than Words"), his English teachers for making school a little more fun, Devon, Aleya, Darren, and Dylan V. for putting up with him, Mr. Curley for believing in this story, "The Art Kids" for giving him something to do during lunch and Lisa for making him take his first steps into a larger world.

The story takes place in a day in the life of a group of apocalypse survivors in Seattle. Throughout the story, two of the survivors go on the weekly shopping trip, engage in conversation, tell a bit of back story, and are confronted by an "Animal". Imagine *Clerks* crossed with *I Am Legend*.

Christian Phillips
Project Reason
Samuel Robertson Technical Secondary School (Grade Eleven)
Maple Ridge, British Columbia
Christian Phillips is sixteen-years-old and lives in Maple Ridge. He enjoys drawing and digital painting. He likes writing, but drawing is his real hobby. He did this story for an English project. The Game.
His inspiration for this story was from his beliefs in God and his faith of God's great power. The story takes place in a time of religious suppression, pre-revelation era. The setting is from his interpretation of Revelation in the New Testament. The main character is meant to be average but dynamic.

April Johnson
Runaway DNA
Samuel Robertson Technical Secondary School (Grade Twelve)
Maple Ridge, British Columbia
April Johnson is an aspiring artist and writer, born on March 24th, 1991. Her focus is on becoming a professional digital artist working in the gaming industry, including that of a

creative professional photographer and music composer. She has played guitar since the age of six and over the years has also acquired the conditional black belt level in Tae Kwon Do. She has lived in Maple Ridge all her life and wishes to travel abroad. Writing has always intrigued her and she continually improves her craft. Her early love for drawing and illustrating, combined with exposure to the computer and technology while very young, has led April to her path.

The story revolves around the controversial issue of Genetically Modified Foods being infiltrated into our consumption and food chain. Much of our agriculture has been monopolized by giant corporations and the pharmaceutical industry with the bottom line in mind. Without our knowing, they can also affect our future health. Although abridged into a short story, these concerns are real as they are currently happening. Many unexplained illnesses and symptoms are showing up, changing our genetics along the way. Beware of what you eat!

Josephine Appeng
The Singing Lark
Samuel Robertson Technical Secondary School (Grade Eleven)
Maple Ridge, British Columbia

Josephine Appeng is seventeen-years-old and currently in grade eleven. She was born in California and moved to Canada when she was eight-years-old. For four years, she lived in Calgary and then moved to British Columbia. Her writing skills were quite mediocre before, and didn't mature until mid-year in grade seven and eight. Writing stories are like playing a movie in her mind. The thesaurus is her best friend when writing, and through it she has learned a wide range of vocabulary. Music is a huge factor that influences her writing, and she listens to whatever helps develop the mood or plot. Her favourite genres are usually: mystery, psychological, drama, some fantasy, and romance; just fiction in general. Other facts about Josephine are: she wants to go to university; she likes to draw, sing, read, run, and play games, shopping, photography, Anime and a variety of foods. Her favourite music genres are: hip-hop, some rap, R&B, rock, pop (English and Asian) and DDR.

She was primarily inspired by tragic stories because they leave a bigger impression. For once, she felt she should write a futuristic story, and had the physical and some emotional setting laid out already in her mind. She tends to include at least one girl and one boy, so her two characters are really close friends living a subtle life in an advanced, metropolitan world. She wanted it to be a somewhat melancholic story, about two small figures fighting for survival against a prominent society, and the environment. A literary term she added was symbolism. The story has scientific matters, which is a huge aspect that revolves around the characters and the plot. Civilization dwells in the sky, and although everything is more sophisticated, humans continue to make mistakes in attempt to perfect life.

Dylan Collier
Tracker
Samuel Robertson Technical Secondary School (Grade Eleven)
Maple Ridge, British Columbia

Dylan was born and grew up in Ontario. He's only recently moved to British Columbia, but he has to say, he really loves both places. The friends he grew up with will never leave his life and the friends he's gained here won't either, good friendships are hard to find, but his are the best. He'd describe himself as a regular teenager; he hangs out with friends, plays video games, watches T.V. and reads.

Tracker is about a world where everyone is being watched, a sad reality that we may actually have to face one day. Jack Bolton is one of the few, if any, "free man" left and he takes it upon himself to undo the "Theorists" no matter the cost. Jack is an intelligent tech-savvy rogue. With the help of an old friend, a new friend, and his own wits, he goes against the odds to fight a major corporation, the new government, while under their watch.

Christian Wahl
Virtual Artificial Intelligence
Samuel Robertson Technical Secondary School (Grade Twelve)
Maple Ridge, British Columbia

Christian was born in Calgary in 1991 on July 16th. He was raised in and around Calgary moving around a lot until he turned eleven. At that point issues with the family had him moving to Vancouver for a fresh start. It was successful and he's happy in his new home. He's a technophile who can't stop tweaking his computer and the software on it. He loves modding and the internet is his playground and his school away from school. He guesses it's ironic that despite being tied to technology so much that he participates in the creation of The Fall-Out. But hey, he can't argue with the value of a good life lesson.

Virtual Artificial Intelligence is about a young guy who's become something of a technology prodigy. He's a genius with computers and lives with a laptop on hand. From his early years he was hacking into restricted web-space and up to nothing but trouble, even if he never really caused much harm. During the time the book takes place, mankind is in a sort of cold war with a nomadic alien race. Technology has surged ahead as a result of the contact and the government is using virtual intelligence computers to train soldiers in combat situations. Unfortunately, the technology is unstable and when one goes rogue, the government is helpless to stop it. In an attempt to salvage the situation quietly, the government makes a deal with Kyle, our hero. In exchange for his help, the government agrees to wipe his criminal record clean.

Ryan Anderson
Wager of Worlds
Samuel Robertson Technical Secondary School (Grade Twelve)
Maple Ridge, British Columbia
Ryan Anderson is in grade twelve. He currently lives in Maple Ridge. He is a major hockey fan. He lives hockey. He plays hockey. He talks hockey. He doesn't write hockey, though. He is a male. He likes the word "Refrain." He has the singing voice of an angel. He has a backpack. He owns five-hundred and fifty five different hockey jerseys. He can roller blade. His future career is a lawyer.
The story takes place in the year 2035. It is the beginning and the end of WWIII between the United States of America and Russia. It informs the reader of the events leading up to the war and the events leading to its finish.

Chayla Port
The "X" Generation
Samuel Robertson Technical Secondary School (Grade Twelve)
Maple Ridge, British Columbia

Comedian. It is a word that Chayla Port would use to describe herself and her future career: A stand-up comic like Jerry Seinfeld. When that doesn't pan out, she will rely on Plan B. Her influences are: Malin Akerman, Bob Dylan, James Franco, Cormac McCarthy, Jim Morrison, Seth Rogen, Paul Rudd, Jerry Seinfeld, and Jason Segel. Both the novel and the film of Watchmen had a huge impact on her life. It's her favourite, highly recommended. Converse is her shoe. The 70's and 80's are her times. She wears glasses and contacts, but not at the same time. She takes major pride in being a unique individual, and works very hard to maintain that status.

The "X" Generation focuses on how people are easily willing to give up their rights and freedoms to have a piece of technology that allows them to live longer. It revolves around the character Jack Callahan, an older man who was imprisoned before society drastically changed. When he is released without approval, he must try to adjust to the new world and piece his life back together. Reuniting with his lost love Evelyn was the beginning, but she has other plans for him…

OUT-TAKES

OUT-TAKES

Printed in the United States
153570LV00001B/2/P